YOU MUST MARKET YOUR BOOK

INCREASE YOUR IMPACT, SELL MORE BOOKS, AND MAKE MORE MONEY

HONORÉE CORDER
AUTHOR, *YOU MUST WRITE A BOOK*

YOU
MUST
MARKET
YOUR BOOK

Increase Your Impact, Sell More Books, and Make More Money

Faster and easier than you ever thought possible, even if you don't have a platform, social media following, or email list

HONORÉE CORDER

ALSO BY HONORÉE CORDER

THE *YOU MUST* BOOK BUSINESS SERIES

- *I Must Write My Book:*
  The Companion Workbook to You Must Write a Book
- *You Must Market Your Book:*
  Increase Your Impact, Sell More Books, and Make More Money
- *I Must Market My Book:*
  The Companion Workbook to You Must Market Your Book
- *You Must Monetize Your Book* (September 2023)
- *I Must Monetize My Book* (September 2023)

OTHER BOOKS & SERIES

- *Business Dating: Applying Relationship Rules*
  in Business for Ultimate Success
- *Tall Order: Organize Your Life*
  and Double Your Success in Half the Time
- *Vision to Reality: How Short Term Massive Action*
  Equals Long Term Maximum Results
- *The Divorced Phoenix: Rising from the Ashes*
  of a Broken Marriage
- *If Divorce is a Game, These are the Rules:*
  8 Rules for Thriving Before, During and After Divorce
- The *Like a Boss* Book Series
- The *Miracle Morning* Book Series
- The *Prosperity for Writers* Book Series
- The *Successful Single Mom* Book Series

Cover and Interior Design by Dino Marino, www.dinomarino.com.

Hardcover ISBN: 978-1-947665-18-7

Paperback ISBN: 978-1-947665-36-1

e-Book ISBN: 978-1-947665-19-4

TABLE OF CONTENTS

Introduction i

CHAPTER ONE
Where Book Marketing Really Begins...1

CHAPTER TWO
Book Marketing from 30,000 Feet 8

CHAPTER THREE
The BEST Book Marketing Starts Here 20

CHAPTER FOUR
Successful Authors Have a Team..24

CHAPTER FIVE
Successful Authors Have Big Plans!..31

CHAPTER SIX
Tools & Other Book Marketing Necessities 55

CHAPTER SEVEN
Today, Tomorrow & the Future...70

CHAPTER EIGHT

Distribution, Sales & Selling.......................................82

CHAPTER NINE

Marketing *with* Your Book.......................................93

CHAPTER TEN

Improvise, Adapt & Overcome..................................99

CHAPTER ELEVEN

Book Marketing Challenge.....................................105

Author's Notes 108

Quick Favor...111

Gratitude 112

Who is Honorée Corder?.......................................115

SPECIAL INVITATION

I'd like to personally invite you to download the book marketing resources I include in this book, including a sample Book Marketing Action Plan and more!

Just visit: HonoreeCorder.com/MarketingBonuses

INTRODUCTION

Dear Reader,

Welcome to *You Must Market Your Book*, the follow-up to *You Must Write a Book*, published, as of this writing, just over six years ago.

A lot has happened in these past six years. Not just for my business, but also in the world. Yet the book itself wouldn't have had the impact it did without consistent, intentional book *marketing*.

The truth is that most of the books that are published sell an average of just 250 books over the course of their *lifetime*. Why?

I believe it's because authors assume a few things:

- *Their book will "automagically" sell once it's published, and*
- *Their publisher will "make" it sell (more magic) with little or no action on their part (or they rely on PR to encourage more than enough sales), and*
- *The heavy lifting is done during the writing and publishing process.*

There are a few other assumptions, and sadly, none of them happen.

Books only sell with a persistent, consistent focus on marketing by the author.

If you have one, your publisher's sole job is in their title—it is to *publish* a quality book for you. True, the writing process can be a challenge, and professionally publishing is critical to a book's chances for success.

Once you have your book in your hot little hands, the fun is only beginning! Yes, I do actually mean *fun*. Book marketing can be a blast. Stay with me; I will get into this later in the book.

The good news is your book need not languish in obscurity—it can, instead, find itself in the four corners of the earth, making connections you might never have made otherwise. Not only can it bring avalanches of revenue to you and your business, but it can also unleash other amazing opportunities and blessings.

Although there is really no way to predict every good thing that will happen, kindly indulge me just a moment while I recount what's happened since I published *You Must Write a Book* in October 2016:

- *(Consider this a foreshadowing for your book as well. The possibilities are endless. YOU can do this too!) I sold over 50,000 copies within a few short months of its release.*

  I'll preface this by saying I had "an in." Amazon had invited me to attend a media breakfast in New York City in the summer of 2016 to highlight the benefits of the KDP platform to the media and help aspiring authors discover and utilize it.

  At the last minute, they canceled the breakfast. I was bummed, but they were going to promote my most recent book, which then was *The Divorced Phoenix: Rising from the Ashes of a Broken Marriage.*

  While I was excited to have the power of Amazon behind my book (any book!), I'm not an expert on divorce. Emphasis on that book for book sales' sake would've been great, but not practical, considering my focus was on writing and publishing books.

So, the entire time I was preparing to go to New York, I wished I had a "better" book for the event. I'd been thinking about writing a book about writing a book, but the timeline was short. However, once the breakfast was rescheduled, I asked if such a book would be welcomed, and I got an enthusiastic *yes.*

With less than 90 days to the October event, I got to work writing *You Must Write a Book.*

I also got to work using the tools I will share in this book.

With my Advanced Reader Team in place, I launched the book, and within 30 days, I was featured in *Fortune Business* (online), *The Huffington Post*, and on dozens of podcasts.

By Christmas, I'd done over 100 podcasts, sent thousands of emails (to grow my email list), and signed and sent over 250 copies to past clients, current clients, and prospective clients. I had price promotions, taking advantage of the benefits of being in KDP Select. Pricing my book at 99 cents in concert with BookBub sent sales soaring. I did everything I could think of to promote the book. By the spring of 2017, I'd sold more than 50,000 copies in all versions.

And I share all my not-so-secret strategies with you throughout this book.

- *After all of that excitement, there were immediate, multiple requests for a workbook to help aspiring authors manage their book projects, so I released I Must Write MY Book Workbook in March 2017.*

- *In addition, after fielding more than two dozen emails asking, "Is there a course for this?" I began teaching Publishing Ph.D. (originally and horribly titled "The You Must Write a Book LIVE! Coaching Course"), helping professionals and entrepreneurs all over the world go from "pen to published." The course is now a blended-learning experience for students (with more than 300 graduates), many of whom join the monthly live Q&A to have me answer their questions.*

- *In 2019, I began the Empire Builders Mastermind, which provides mentorship and a positive environment for entrepreneurs who want to create additional income streams, with at least one originating from their book. In 2023, I am hosting it for the fifth year in a row, and with 13 participants, I'm able to provide real-time personal guidance to each member.*

- *In early 2020, I released another course, Building a Million Dollar Book Business, to help students repurpose their content into other income streams.*

- *And finally, I've produced over a dozen books for business owners and entrepreneurs who reached out, stating they had "more money than time" and wanted to outsource the entire process.*

All told, I've made several million dollars as a result of writing, publishing, selling, and marketing *You Must Write a Book*. For clarity, I self-published the book, did not hire a PR firm or marketing agency, and didn't work more than 40 hours in any one week.

I share all of this with you so you can see that a book can be both a source of income from book sales and also naturally result in additional income streams.

But this isn't about me, so I'll gratefully change the subject back to you and your book—and all of its potential!

What you need to do is focus on the steady marketing of your book and analyze each new opportunity and idea in the process. It's easier said than done, which is why I wrote this book: so you can enjoy the fruits of your labor in easy, lucrative, and fun ways.

Said another way, I want you to have a checklist of book marketing "to do" items housed in a solid Book Marketing Action Plan (your Book MAP). I also want you to understand how to *think* about book marketing so you get the most out of every single action you take.

WHAT IS BOOK MARKETING?

Book marketing is an author's strategic execution of identifying and appealing to prospective readers (and can include advertising, branding, pricing, and sales).

Said more simply, book marketing is connecting one's book to readers.

But make no mistake—book marketing and other product or service marketing aren't exactly the same. Sure, some of the fundamentals are the same or similar, yet the differences could actually determine a book's success or failure.

It is many times assumed that if someone understands marketing, nay, they are marketing experts, then they have a firm handle on book marketing as well. While they are probably better equipped than most authors, there is a distinction with a difference.

So why exactly is book marketing different? I'm so glad you asked!

While the investment for a book is a few dollars and is usually considered minimal (certainly compared to hiring an author to provide the same information one-on-one), it is time-consuming to read a book. The real investment you're asking for when marketing and selling your book is *time*. Most people look at a book and ask themselves, *Am I going to get a solid return on investment for the time I spend reading this book? Does it solve my problem, help me to do something better, or help me get something I want?*

In addition, prospective readers of your book have thousands of choices and almost as many options for other things to do besides read.

Marketing a stereo, vacation, or new car is different because the time investment required for the buyer is significant.

While almost everyone watches television, listens to music, and needs a new pair of pants each season, no one really *has* to read your book.

Read that again.

Reading your book isn't essential. That is, unless you make it compelling to do so.

Your book marketing game has to be tight because not only must you inspire someone to invest their money, but they also need to have some urgency around taking the time to read it.

When it comes to nonfiction books, and that's the focus of our discussion in this book, you, the author, have a twofold intent for a segment of your readers. Right? You want them to benefit from your knowledge *and* engage with you at a deeper level.

If they don't read your book, the chances are they won't engage.

Thus, your marketing must compel them to buy and *read*.

After all, what you really want people to do is read and love your book. Right? (Yes, me too!)

I understand these are seemingly insurmountable hurdles, but I've got you! My entire reason for writing this book is to help you understand book marketing—not just what to do, but where, when, and *why*—as well as empower you with the ability to craft and execute a book marketing plan that does everything you need it to do.

Whether you are still working on your book or you published a book five years ago, within these pages, you'll find effective tactics to help you market your book and insight into the strategic thinking that will help your book continue to sell and sell and sell in the years to come.

Grab a journal (or a copy of *I Must Market MY Book Workbook*) and a pen, and let's begin.

Honorée Corder
Honorée Enterprises Publishing
1890 Fairview Blvd., Box 333
Fairview, Tennessee 37062
USA

CHAPTER ONE

WHERE BOOK MARKETING REALLY BEGINS

Books sell not by chance but through purposeful, intentional, and consistent marketing.

You can be a literal book marketing genius, super ninja. Still, if you don't have two pivotal components of the book marketing puzzle in place, your book will not sell (sad but true) and will not generate the new business you dream about (also sad and true).

Said another way, you cannot put lipstick on a prizewinning hog and pretend it will be the horse that wins the Kentucky Derby.

So, before I can educate you on the finer points of crafting a book marketing plan that will make all your book marketing and business dreams come true, we have to take a step back and make sure you have your proverbial ducks in a row.

THE TWO VITAL COMPONENTS FOR A BOOK'S SUCCESS

The two components I am referring to are:

- The quality of your book, and
- Your book marketing mindset.

Mindset is so important I'm going to bump it to the top of this short list.

Why?

Because if you don't believe your book can be successful—in the ways you define success for it and yourself—it won't be. You might as well keep doing what you've been doing, *sans* a book.

YOUR BOOK MARKETING MINDSET

Once you have a book, or even before you do, there are many things you can do to capitalize on the benefits of being an author. *(And by capitalize, I mean make money.)*

For now, I want to be sure we set you up for success with your book. Book marketing success is like a marriage: you've got to have a positive attitude going in, or you're doomed from the start.

I would love to abolish the belief that money cannot be made from book sales. In fact, I can attest many people make money from their book. They sell their book by signing and selling books in concert with a speaking engagement and bulk sales, just to name two. They also sell their books through online retailers, in book and big box stores, and in many other ways.

Marketing your book starts with a successful book marketing mindset. I will not spend a ton of time talking about it in this book, but I would be remiss if I didn't bring it to your attention.

You'll know your mindset needs work if you are already arguing with me while you read this … *"But Honorée, my friend Steve published his book, and it hasn't made him any money!"* Or *"Hey, I published a book three years ago and still have eight boxes of it in my garage. Please explain! Do you mean to tell me it's all my fault?"*

Whoa, there. Simmer down. I don't play blame or fault games. But I know this for sure—if someone, *anyone*, and this means you, too, has a book and it is not selling, chances are there is a gap in the marketing plan.

Or the author's mindset game isn't in the right place.

Or the book quality doesn't stand up.

Or all three.

This isn't a book on mindset, but if you want to make sure yours is in order, grab a copy of my book *Prosperity for Writers*. Because before you can see your book become a success, you've got to believe it is going to be one!

For our conversation here—and I hope it's a conversation—I want you to pull out a sticky note. On that sticky note, write the amount of income you want to earn from your book sales and royalties, and how much more you'd like to make from engaging new clients and customers who find you through your book.

I set a goal to earn $100,000 in book sales from my first book, *Tall Order!* After publishing in 2005, I sold 11,000 copies and earned over $100,000 in the first three weeks (I talked about it on the *Author Hour* podcast in 2017) (https://authorhour.co/sell-self-published-book-honoree-corder/). Why? Because I didn't know I wasn't supposed to do that!

What you won't ever hear from me again (other than in the introduction) is how many books the average author sells, or that something (anything!) is impossible. I know you can do it because I did it—and because I'm going to help you do it, too!

THE QUALITY OF YOUR BOOK

The second component of a successful book is the quality of the book.

Just as your hog will not win the Kentucky Derby, a book written in a weekend with a cover designed in Word, that was published on Amazon for 99 cents, that the author told the entire world to buy and review, will not be a best-earning book that boosts your brand, builds your business, and makes you the go-to expert.

Stop to take a breath.

I'm just sayin'!

The Four Cornerstones of a Professionally Published Book are the first, best, and only place to start.

My first goal when publishing a book is not to sell a million copies (that's my second goal). My first goal when publishing a book is to *publish it such that it is indistinguishable from traditional publishing.* Those folks in New York, Chicago, and Los Angeles hold a high bar for books—and theirs is a standard I strive to meet and exceed.

In order to run with the big guys, a book has to have the same feel and read they do. Here are the boxes your book must check to fit in (and stand out) among its peers:

The cover has to be *awesome*. Yes, I know awesome is nebulous, so here are some pointers:

Make it *fit in* and *stand out*. It must look like the other books in your genre, and when possible, just a bit better. Think: so compelling that someone wants to pick it up, flip it over to read the back cover, and buy it and read it (preferably all on the same day). You'll want to hire someone who specializes in book cover design, who understands the difference between RGB and CMYK, and who can produce a clean cover design (not muddy or "self-published looking") (I know you know what I mean!). *Study the other books in your category. What are the themes, colors, and images of the ones that are selling? How can you make your book fit right in among those books?*

The back cover needs excellent copy (more on that below), a professional photo of you with a short bio, the main category of your book, the price, a barcode, and maybe a testimonial or three. *Fire up Amazon and check out the covers of books that are selling well after at least a year (check publication date and sales rank; anything under 30,000 in the Amazon store is a great place to start).*

A quality cover will cost around $1,000, and a custom cover in all formats will run you between $1,500 and $2,000. Before you balk, consider how much clients pay to work with you. One terrific cover can bring new clients *en masse*, making investing in a quality cover a sound investment.

You'll want a next-to-flawless read. This means hiring, at the very least, a professional editor *and* a professional proofreader (maybe two of each if this is your first book). You'll know they are a pro because someone trained them in traditional publishing and they put "editor" or "proofreader" on their tax return.

An edited book that follows a manual of style (such as *The Chicago Manual of Style*) and has been proofread will produce a quality book without typos and misspelled, extra, or missing words. These two passes of your book by professionals will also point out other deficiencies and ensure you give credit where credit is due. They will put a true polish on your manuscript, thus allowing it to do the heavy lifting it is meant to do. (New clients and higher fees, anyone?) While no book is perfect—and no matter how many eyes you have on a book, something is bound to slip through—embracing a thorough editorial process will create an enjoyable, beneficial read for the reader, allowing them to get to know you through your expertise, perhaps turning a prospect into a client. Keep in mind quality editors and proofreaders are in high demand, and you should seek to engage them about three months before you finish your manuscript.

Editors will run 4–8 cents per word, and proofreaders 2–4.5 cents per word. There are fantastic folks available who used to work in trade and are now freelance. You can find some in my Facebook group, the Prosperous Writer Mastermind (you can join it here: https://www.facebook.com/groups/ProsperityforWriters), or through a personal recommendation.

Interior formatting for your e-book and print is mega-important. Clean formatting in an easy-to-read font is a must. You can do a basic format of your book by using a free tool Draft2Digital provides. If your budget allows, engage a custom formatter to add special effects (such as beginning of chapter graphics, icons to drive home your point in certain sections, or even space to do exercises, or a summary of your chapter).

If the goal of your book is to develop new business, I suggest investing in quality, custom formatting to add polish and visual excellence to the interior design. The added value will enhance the knowledge and expertise you share in your book by calling out what readers most need to pay attention to, as well as distill your knowledge into digestible pieces.

The brilliance behind this book's formatting is Dino Marino, find him at DinoMarino.com. You can find my personal other recommendations for formatters in the book's bonuses, or you can try Vellum (www.Vellum.pub), a software you can buy and use for semi-custom formatting.

Front and back matter are additional important elements. They are almost as important as the main content of your book. In the front of your book, be sure to include your table of contents, introduction, and an invitation for folks to join your email list. In the back of your book, share some author's notes about why, where, and when you wrote the book, a bio including a list of your other publications, and any other offerings you have (such as courses, keynote presentations, or even annual live events).

Your book description (a.k.a. sales copy or back cover copy) converts prospective buyers to readers. Your book's description lets a prospective reader understand what the book is about—and you'll want to *for sure* engage a pro to write it for you! Great copy converts at a higher rate than even an exceptional cover, so fork over the few hundred bucks it takes to have an expert *sell your book*.

To write your copy, the copywriter will need some or all of the following:

- Your book's title & subtitle, with
- A 2-sentence "in your own words" overview of your book, and
- The table of contents (with 1–2 sentences about each chapter), and
- Your long bio.

Note: Your book, written in your voice, should sound like you. Right? Your book description *will not sound like you*, and it shouldn't. **The job of sales copy is to sell.** Please don't make the mistake of taking the sales copy you pay for and "making it sound like you." That is a mistake I see authors make. Let the copy do its job, okay? Okay!

To sum up, these are the four cornerstones: **cover, the editorial process** (*including editing and proofreading*)**, interior design** (*also consider the front and back matter*)**,** and **book description.** Doing these well will allow your book to compete with others in your genre—and win! Prospective readers (and clients) won't know it's self-published, and they'll be impressed that you're an author, and that your book is so well done!

I would be remiss if I didn't mention that your book needs to be addressed to the person who should read it. Having an ideal reader in mind (hint: the profile of your ideal reader is identical to that of your ideal client) is key to the book having the true effect you desire.

Now that we've gotten all of *that* established, we can get into the good stuff: how to market your book and market *with* your book.

When you're ready, let's begin!

CHAPTER TWO

BOOK MARKETING FROM 30,000 FEET

Before we can dive into the tactical pieces of book marketing (what you do daily), we must first look at book marketing from a much higher level.

I use the 30,000-foot perspective because, from that height, you can see the entire landscape (how your book fits into your business) and an expanded timeline (how your book can work hard for you for, let's say, a decade to come).

For this book, I'm going to assume you've met the criteria I suggested in Chapter 1. Meaning: you've got a quality book that is a true asset to you and your business, and it can work hard on your behalf.

If so, let's put that kid in action and maximize every aspect of its potential.

STRATEGIC THINKING

Unless you're a *Fortune 500* CEO or have a team around you, you most likely play at least three roles in your business: business development, work product creation, and relationship building.

Ryan Serhant, in his book *Sell It Like Serhant,* calls these roles finder, keeper, and doer.

Your book can immensely assist you in the *finder* department. In fact, if you market your book well, you will see a steady stream of potential client inquiries.

Of course, it is important that I mention you must do great work and provide excellent professional services. A well-crafted book that attracts new clients is only the beginning. It's what the client experiences, from the initial inquiry and throughout their entire engagement, that truly seals the deal.

Do yourself, your business, and your book a favor and implement an incredible customer experience.

I will stop myself from going off on a tangent to discuss the key differences between being a transactional businessperson instead of reaping the rich rewards of being a relationship-focused businessperson. In short, I believe the latter has a much easier time in life and in business. If you want to know more about that, grab a copy of my book on networking and business development, *Business Dating*.

Assuming you have incredible content in your book, and it—and you—deliver "as advertised" (it meets the promise of the title and subtitle, and you are a credit to your profession), I encourage you to look at the role your book can play in your business.

THE ROLE OF YOUR BOOK IN AND FOR YOUR BUSINESS

Your book can wear many hats, and it should.

It can boost your brand—there's almost nothing more powerful than being an author when it comes to establishing credibility.

It can exponentially multiply your business development efforts—a book can open doors, connect you with people you otherwise would not meet, and go places you can't go. (The least of which is that you simply cannot be in two places at once, *but your book can be in thousands of places at the same time.*)

It can position you as the go-to expert in your physical location or area of expertise—once you have the book, you could be the

Dave Ramsey of mental health awareness or the Brené Brown of women's empowerment.

Said another way, your book can do the heavy lifting by raising your profile, increasing your following, and helping probable purchasers feel confident you are "the one" for them.

STRATEGIC THINKING AND THE ROLE OF YOUR BOOK

Your next most obvious step is to decide the role or roles you want the book to play, and then connect the dots to help it do just that.

When you think strategically about your book, and execute accordingly, you will get more of what you want. More business? More income? More freedom? And less of what you don't want. Less business development stress? Less time and money wasted? Less effort for bigger results? All of this and so much more.

Your book will provide line passes and shortcuts to client engagement like almost nothing else can.

As a self-published author, when I published my first books in 2004, 2005, and 2009, I didn't have the supposed marketing engine of a traditional publishing company behind me or access to fancy public relations firms. I did not find myself on the *TODAY* show. (Hi, Hoda!) I also didn't have worldwide distribution when I released a book.

Nor did I have a big pile of cash that allowed me to spend $25,000 a month on said public relations firm, an unlimited travel budget that provided for a book tour (I'm open to spending three months on a fancy tour bus, though ...), etc., and so forth.

All of that to say: I had to think strategically about my book and how I was going to connect it with potential readers.

I had a role for my book to play—I had a *why* behind my *what*: I wanted to develop new business coaching clients and do more training within service firms. With that in mind, I needed to get that book into the hands of as many senior-level business folks as

I could, specifically decision makers at law firms, CPA firms, and other service firms that needed my expertise.

By introducing my process to them and putting a spotlight on my abilities through my book, they could discern whether I might be an excellent coach for them or their company. My book provided insight into not only my method but also the results I'd created with others.

I also had to get scrappy: Without a marketing budget that allowed me to buy expensive swag or sponsor expensive events and dinners, I needed to be creative and innovative in my book marketing.

I took a multi-pronged approach, which included the following:

Study what others are doing. I studied what other published authors were doing, listened to their stories, read their books, and attended their seminars. Okay, *seminar*. There was one seminar: Mega Book Marketing (with Mark Victor Hansen). Today there are dozens, maybe hundreds, of books, author and writer podcasts, and conferences. There is endless information from authors who are marketing their books successfully. You can learn a lot from what other authors are doing. In fact, you'll learn what *to do* and what *not to do*.

You can also connect with local authors, sometimes simply by asking: *Who are my friends who are authors?* Ask your connections on Facebook or conduct a geographical search on LinkedIn to see which of your contacts are also authors. I get some of my best ideas from conversations with other authors.

You can also pull a page out of the playbooks of more well-known authors and performers who are successful at marketing their books, movies, and music.

Will Smith, in his book *Will*, talked about how he studied what the four biggest movie stars in the world did to hold that position of "the biggest movie star in the world." All household names, beloved by millions, when Will asked them how he, too, could become mega-successful, they told him he had to shake every hand, attend every event, and kiss every baby. Oh, and stay until the very last person has met you, shook your hand, and told you why they love your work. Now I'm paraphrasing here, but not terribly much. Will wanted to be the biggest star in the world, and he set about doing the work one day at a time and building his brand one fan at a time. (Oh, and if you haven't read his book, I highly recommend you do so by listening to the audiobook, which he narrates brilliantly.)

In 1996, Garth Brooks signed autographs for 23 straight hours at Fan Fair (now CMA Fest). We know Supermodel Tyra Banks for her charity work. Keanu Reeves is one of the nicest guys ever, with a long list of fan encounters (he even gave a $20,000 bonus to a set employee on *The Matrix* because they were having family problems).

Here's where I get to give a hat-tip to authors who have been exceptional and kind to me (and I have it on good authority I'm far from the only one): Deborah Coonts was one of the first authors I met just after the publication of her first book, *Wanna Get Lucky?* Jeff Goins and I have become good friends, and I was first a fan of his work. J. T. Ellison and I first crossed paths at WriterFest in Nashville a few years ago, and we chat occasionally. All three are brilliant writers and wonderful humans, and they are just three of many examples.

Does their "offstage" behavior contribute to their success? I'm going to say a resounding *yes*.

It doesn't take but a few times for someone to seem too big for their britches to kill any momentum they've gained. I could make a list of "whatever happened to ..." artists, and you'd see what I mean.

All of that to say, at the very top of your list of "things that successful authors do," is *to be nice*.

I have two things to say before we move past the subject of listening to what others are sharing:

<u>One</u>. Carefully vet someone before you take their advice. There are some fame addicts out there who love the spotlight and get it as soon and as often as they can. Some are authentically selling

lots of books and sharing valuable content. Some are not. Do your due diligence.

Two. It is easy to get overwhelmed by the abundance of information that's being shared. While I make it a point to uncover and discover what's out there, I also take time to carefully consider what makes sense to me. More on that later; I really just wanted to point that out for you.

Then do what they are doing ... There are the fundamental, tried-and-true book marketing tactics that work. Ultimately, there are fundamentals that can work if you apply them and apply them consistently. They aren't sexy, and they aren't exciting, but they will work. Having foundational elements in your book marketing that have been around the block a few times and are still connecting books to readers is an excellent idea.

... and (just maybe) do the opposite. I also read (and still read) books on creativity and innovative thinking. There are more today than there were in 2004 and 2005, and I've got a list for you at HonoreeCorder.com/myfavoritebooks (look under Productivity and Creativity). Both Lady Gaga and Madonna are famous for zigging while others are zagging. When "everyone" is doing TikTok or BookTok videos (at the time of this writing, that is all the rage), you will want to put on your cynical glasses and see whether you really want to make videos (including edit, set to music, add subtitles, etc.) on the regular. If you do, fantastic. Do it; have fun with it! If not, take a pass.

I'm going into much more detail later in the book, but let me put this question here (and yes, I know it is common sense, but have you been doing it?) to have in your left front pocket to use every day from this day forward:

Is what you're doing working? This is the million-dollar book marketing question. The fundamentals that work for James Patterson and the TikTok videos that put nine of Colleen Hoover's books on the *New York Times* Bestseller List (also as of this writing) may or may not work for you and your book.

FINAL NOTE

Commit and hold steady. My last thought on this is: You must commit to a strategy and engage the tactics long enough to actually know whether they are working.

I used to love coming up with a new idea, then going down a rabbit hole. I'd be so excited to create a new profile and post 74 things over the first few days. Then it wasn't long before I'd get bored, didn't feel like giving whatever I was doing the attention it needed, and then (here's the shocker) it didn't work. Hmm.

Wisdom and experience (okay, wasted time and money *plus* wisdom and experience) have brought me to the place where I gather all the information I can. Then I take a step back to create a strategic, thoughtful plan that fits me, my business, and my book.

From this point forward, my intention and goal are to provide you with exactly what you need to market your book, a potentially magical combination of strategy and tactics plus creative thinking and intuition.

You don't just want to be *monogamous with Amazon* without knowing why and even for how long. It makes little sense to publish on Amazon at all if you're focused on developing business solely in your zip code. I will talk more about this in Chapter 8.

Learning how to *think* strategically will allow you to market your book strategically. To capture ideas, process them thoughtfully, and then take deliberate action designed to move you closer to your goals and objectives.

It's important for the long-term success of your book that you not only take massive action, but you understand why you're doing what you're doing, know how long you're going to do it, and measure whether it is working.

Once you've pinpointed how your book fits into your business, you can develop your strategic book marketing plan. There's one more key element to know before you plan.

THE 80/20 RULE OF BOOK MARKETING

I'm sure you've heard of the Pareto principle, which is defined as *for many outcomes, roughly 80% of the consequences come from 20% of the causes*. I'm a positive thinker, so let's exchange *consequences* for *results*.

So, 80% of your book marketing results are going to come from 20% of your actions. At least initially.

Whether you've published and marketed 10 books, or this is your first go-around, you're going to have a learning curve. Every book, author, date of release, and even the reader bench is different. What worked swimmingly well for your first book may fall flat for your second or seventeenth.

Paying attention to what gets meaningful results and what doesn't is key.

Eventually, you'll be able to narrow it down so that 100% of your results come from doing a few intentional marketing actions regularly.

Regular analysis of your book marketing efforts will help you stop doing what doesn't work and double down on what does. You'll figure out the three, five, or seven activities that bring readers into your ecosystem, and you can do them over, and over, and over. And let go of the rest.

JUST BECAUSE "EVERYONE" IS DOING IT ...

Case in point: If you're fairly outgoing and passionately love to talk about your book, being a podcast guest can be a terrific way to put fresh eyes on your book and your brand. This describes me to a T, so I've been a guest on hundreds of podcasts.

I recently helped a client who is a self-described introvert publish a book. He hated the idea of being on podcasts and had the smallest book launch "party" in history (six family members, me, and his ghostwriter). I mean, *he doesn't even like to leave his house more than once a week to go out to eat.* In-tro-vert, kids, in-tro-vert! When I suggested talking about his book on podcasts and in the media, he looked back at me without saying a word, but the message was clear by the look on his face. *Doing that sounded like less fun than getting a root canal.* I could tell we needed to address his book marketing in other, creative ways. And we did.

I don't have permission to share the plan we came up with, but I share most of the strategies within the pages of this book. I can't imagine there isn't someone reading this who's going: *This is me!* So, I share this example because just because something works amazingly well for most others, if you don't want to do it (with one or every fiber of your being), don't feel you have to. You'll just put your ninja book marketing thinking cap on and come up with other ways to market your book.

The 80/20 Rule of Book Marketing is something to keep in mind when you're brainstorming your Book Marketing Action Plan.

ENTER: THE BOOK MARKETING ACTION PLAN

Everything I've written up to this point was to help prepare you for putting together your Book Marketing Action Plan (your MAP).

If you've just skipped to this section, I get you. I always want the fast pass to results, too. Keep reading, but before you put pen to paper, take a few minutes and start at the beginning of the book, so you're really ready for what you're doing. Also, note: This is just an overview. I revisit these concepts and dive deeper into them in Chapter 5.

BOOK MARKETING-IN-ACTION

This is a short section designed to help you nail down your initial time and monetary commitments.

You're a busy professional, already using every hour of every day to grow your business.

Besides understanding yourself and acknowledging your personality, there are two questions to ask before filling out the rest of your MAP:

1. How are you going to find time to market?
2. Also, you've got some money to spend on promotion and marketing, but how much?

While you build out a comprehensive plan, the time and monetary limitations you have will inform and influence your execution. Keeping the 80/20 Rule in mind—I'm going to say this is a great thing—the less time and money you have to throw at your book, the more intentional you'll need to be when choosing, evaluating, and adjusting later.

THE BOOK MARKETING MATRIX

The Book Marketing Matrix (called just the "Matrix," and not to be confused with anything the aforementioned Keanu Reeves is doing) is the foundation of your overall Book MAP.

The Book Marketing Matrix consists of four columns, 10 possibilities for each column, that provide certainty your book's success *will not be left to chance.* You won't wake up every day frozen in fear, wondering what on earth you should do to market your book.

You'll have designed the four aspects of your book marketing based on these categories:

- Publish & Repurpose: *How will you publish your book (what formats), and how will you repurpose the content into other formats and/or marketing efforts?*
- Distribution: *How and where can readers buy your book?*
- Promotion: *What will you do to connect your book, in all the formats you've chosen, with prospective readers?*
- Selling: *How and where will you actually sell your book?*

Publish & Repurpose	Distribution	Promotion	Selling
E-book	Amazon	ADS: AMS + BookBub	1-1
Paperback	Draft2Digital	Podcasts*	1-many (bulk)***
Hardcover (case laminate/SE)	Kobo	Summits	Special editions via website
Audio (Rob Actis)	iBooks	Other author promos (BookFunnel)	Sales (Black Friday)
YouTube readings (one chapter at a time / select segments)	IngramSpark (h/c + bulk)	Social Media**	Speaking Engagements (back of the room sales)
Companion: *I Must Market MY Book* (1/2023)	Findaway Voices (audio)	Newsletter via email / LinkedIn	Author Conferences* (sponsorship tables)
March is National "Market Your Book" Month	Big Box (Target / Walmart)	Networking (local)	Bulk direct
Gift: Buy the book for an author you love!	Indie / Local Bookstores	Networking (author buddies)	Bulk via distributor (limited consignment)
Book Marketing Mastery Course	Specialty Shops (w/YMWAB)	Networking (targeted)	Foreign translations
Book Marketing Mastery Strategy Sessions	Self / website	Postcards (direct mail)	Other****

*Podcast List, Author Conferences (see Book MAP)
**Social Media for this book: Instagram, LinkedIn, Facebook
***Hybrid publishers, book coaches, +++.
****see Book MAP

As you can see, I am not leaving my book's success to chance. I've used my experience to design a Matrix to market this book, and before I continue, would you take one minute and send me an email at Honoree@HonoreeCorder.com and tell me how you discovered this book?

Once you've decided on your time and monetary commitments and completed your Matrix, then you can complete your Book MAP.

This plan houses every aspect of the future of your book marketing.

- Book Marketing Pre-Launch Plan. Here's where you'll describe how you're going to put rocket boosters on your book prior to launch. *This includes forming and working with your advanced reader team and deciding on your retail platforms. This is a part of my overall publishing strategy and the entire overview isn't included in this book. You can read about it in* You Must Write a Book *and learn about it in my course: Publishing Ph.D.* I'll share a bit about it in Chapter 5.

- Book Marketing during Launch Days 1–30. *Getting the proper lift-off for your book is key. Your activities in this first month can make all the difference in the following months and even years.* You'll learn how and what to do, and who you need to help you in Chapter 5.

- Book Marketing Day 31–Forever. *Done properly, you can pare down to the bare minimum in your activities and reap huge results.* Learn how to analyze and adjust your marketing for short-, medium-, and long-term book marketing in Chapter 5.

- Book Marketing Action Item Checklist. *With a comprehensive list of actions combined with your savvy and smarts, you can almost guarantee your book's success.* In Chapter 5, I prime the pump with ideas you'll love.

- Connections, Networking, and Building Relationships. *Ideas for connecting with influencers for single book sales and bulk orders abound so that you can keep the love for your book alive and not lose that loving feeling.* Chapter 6 is all about keeping your momentum and diversifying.

- Book Social Media Action Plan. *No book marketing plan would be complete without a social media presence.* I'm going to help you cut through the noise and make the most of the free social media sites in Chapter 5.

As you can see, with your very own MAP, you have a comprehensive plan for getting eyes on your book and your business. You'll know what to do and when to do it, and you'll have confidence.

You can find a blank, downloadable Book Marketing Action Plan at HonoreeCorder.com/MarketingBonuses. If you want to take this process step-by-step, be sure to grab the companion *I Must Market MY Book Workbook.* You can also take my course Book Marketing Mastery by visiting HonoreeCorder.com/Marketing (use the code READER to get a generous discount on the course as well).

Now you've got an overview of what goes into your MAP, it's time to go through it while I teach you how to think it through—not just fill in some blank lines. I want you to understand what goes into it, where, and why. I also want you to have a true understanding of how to think creatively in your book marketing.

I'm ready when you are.

CHAPTER THREE

THE BEST BOOK MARKETING STARTS HERE

When creating your MAP (how I'll refer from now on to your Book Marketing Action Plan), I've got two different things to keep in mind:

One. Your Avatar (Ideal Reader) is Everything: Effective book marketing means focusing solely on the ideal reader for your book.

I know it might seem like I'm taking steps backward, especially if you've already published your book. However, the truth bears repeating: Having a quality book is critical, as is knowing exactly who is going to read and benefit from reading the book.

In *You Must Write a Book*, I talk about knowing exactly who your book is for—who can and should read your book—and tailoring your content only for them.

It makes sense then, doesn't it, that you focus your book marketing in the same direction?

If you didn't read *You Must Write a Book*, and you've already published your book (and even if you haven't), consider this:

No book is for "everyone." A writer is well-served to write to a well-defined reader. A book marketer is well-served to market to that same well-defined reader.

Further, *when you direct your focus, you'll get better results coming and going!*

When deciding your overall strategy, followed by specific tactics, always keep your avatar clearly in mind.

Then, any time and every time you are thinking of including something in your overall strategy, ask yourself key questions like these:

- Will your avatar watch *Good Morning America* hoping for a book recommendation?

- Would the person who engages you most often take a recommendation from their dentist, priest, or business attorney?

- Are you hired to speak by meeting planners who listen to podcasts?

Something may sound like a terrific idea: "Yeah, I'll rent a billboard on I-40! Tens of thousands of commuters will see my book and buy it!" But when you get down to it, *will they?*

Is your prospective reader likely to pick up what you're putting down where you're putting it down? (Said another way, will your best prospective readers find your book where you're sharing or advertising it?)

Just a few quality questions can save you mountains of time and money.

Two. The BEST Book Marketing Strategies. Use the BEST Book Marketing Strategies to direct your marketing efforts, so you can attract book sales rather than recruiting or forcing them.

I've created the acronym BEST so you can keep these strategies in mind while you're constructing your plan.

B is for Business-centered. Your book boosts your brand and helps you generate new business. Every aspect of your marketing strategies and tactics needs to drive prospective readers to become probable purchasers.

If you are considering adding something to your MAP, but it doesn't fit with the way your ideal reader is likely to discover your book, make it a hard pass.

If you're unsure, put it on a separate "maybe" list to use another time.

E is for Executing with Intention and Purpose. This is big! Identifying actions for your plan is one thing; knowing you want to and can execute it with intention and purpose is quite another.

Do you *want* to do it? Does it fit with your introverted, extroverted, or ambiverted personality? Yes? Okay, good.

Can you do it, i.e., do you have the time and money? Yes? Keep going.

Can you be intentional about it, meaning, can you consistently execute it until you can evaluate whether it's working?

Does it serve your purpose? Does it connect your book with readers who then read your book and hire or buy from you?

When evaluating tactics and answering these questions, go with the ones you can put a strong yes behind. If you're wishy-washy or don't feel good, maybe note it for another time.

S is for Strategic. Strategic is a follow-up to E. I like my actions to be strategic from multiple perspectives: Does it help my reader in a positive way, does it help my brand in a positive way, and does it contribute to my bottom line? Those are just three options.

Being strategic means you're looking at the bigger picture, the longer timeline, rather than just doing something for the sake of doing it, or for a short-term gain.

T is for Timely. Does it make sense to do it now, later, or both?

Renting a billboard might make sense for your book (it doesn't, but stay with me here), but at $25,000 a month for one billboard, you're going to need some serious cash flow to justify allocating $300,000 under a year's contract toward one book marketing tactic. Let's do some simple math: to break even an investment of

$300,000, you'd have to sell 60,000 books at $5 *profit. Just to break even.* We can't even consider what the return on your investment might be, but I doubt it would be impressive.

Always consider the potential return on investment before you spend even one dollar or minute of your time, even if you have an abundance of both.

As you put together your MAP, compare every action against these criteria. Your *best* book marketing needs to meet or exceed the BEST Book Marketing criteria test.

With those thoughts in mind, let's go to the next level in our discussion about your book marketing success.

CHAPTER FOUR

SUCCESSFUL AUTHORS HAVE A TEAM

By now, I hope you're filled with positive anticipation—the beginning of a true understanding of how to market (and sell) your book. So you can generate new business? Grow an additional income stream? Be a full-time Authorpreneur? Leave an otherwise lucrative career you're not in love with? It doesn't matter! I want you to feel enthusiastic instead of anxious, eager instead of restless, delighted instead of distressed—always—when you think about what's ahead for you and your book.

This chapter holds four more dependable procedures that will exponentially multiply your marketing efforts. That's a big promise, and I'm ready to deliver.

Let's go!

"Who is on my team, HC?"

A fine question, asked to me by every author I've worked with.

You might assume your book's success is up to more than just you, right?

Do you want the good news or the bad news first?

The bad news? Oh—well, there's no bad news—only good news and reality news.

The Reality News First:

Your book marketing team consists foremost of *you*.

When a blockbuster movie is released, the movie's star must go on a press junket, make the rounds, and answer the same questions repeatedly.

They can't send their stunt double to do the most important work after the film wraps. They must market the movie, and they do. Without their full participation, the movie will flop. With their participation, people line up to buy popcorn (extra fake butter, please!) and peanut M&M's (or is that just me?) and watch the movie.

I mentioned Will Smith and every other well-known performer knows this, and they execute on it. Being the face of your book, and your author brand, is just part of the job. In fact, it is Job One right behind writing the book.

On a side note, I'm so excited I can rent new releases right from the comfort of my home, real butter, comfy sweats, and all!

Remember: As an author, marketing your book is no different. Many authors want to outsource their marketing. If I had a dollar for every time I've heard "I'll just hire a PR firm!" and "My publisher will handle that," I could have a sweet flat in Paris.

Ask any traditionally published author who is tasked with doing their book marketing, and you'll get the same answer: "Me." Many an author has thought someone else would do it, only to learn (the painful way) that wasn't the case.

You, my friend, are the engine of the entire operation. I want you to prepare yourself to do an Ultraman (basically a triple IRONMAN triathlon). If you were going to do the equivalent of three rounds of running a marathon, swimming a 5K, and biking 112 miles, you'd put on some great music, wear comfortable shoes, and pack delicious snacks.

You'd also do a ton of training. The good news is your training consists of preparing your MAP—you won't even break a sweat!

You must prepare yourself to market your book. Unless the content in your book is time-limited (i.e., *"How to survive the last three months of 2020"*), you should be able to market and sell your book for at least a decade. The great news? Your book can sell more year-over-year if you stay focused on marketing it. It isn't an avocado; after all, it doesn't go bad. You have a limitless supply of potential readers.

Every morning, ask yourself, "What can I do, and what can be done, to market my book today?" Then, consult your MAP, and you'll know what to do, when, and why.

"Anyone else?"

Are you clear now that you must lead the charge on book marketing? Okay, good. Time for more good news. Now I feel comfortable sharing who else can be on your bench with you.

I can see you're holding your breath, hoping there is at least some of the enormous pile of marketing work that other folks could do.

Yes, yes, there is.

They are self-explanatory, and we have a long way to go, so I'll keep it simple:

- **An assistant.** Having a great assistant, especially one who can book podcasts and speaking gigs, create images for your social media (as well as handle the media side of your social media … more on that later in Chapter 5), and send out emails to your readership, is a godsend. One tip here: hire for attitude, train for skill.

- **A social media marketing firm or manager.** Social media channels change almost daily, and new "must-do" applications appear almost daily. If you have the budget, explore your options. One tip here: ask for proof of results from other authors *just like you*. (Results from fiction authors or experts in other fields won't cut it.)

- **A PR firm or media expert.** I'm unconvinced an expensive PR firm provides the return on investment for books that it does for other entertainment mediums. However, if you have the budget, knock yourself out. Even as a seven-figure earner, I don't enjoy the thought of lighting a brick of money on fire just to see how fast it'll burn. Being more of a scrappy nature myself, I like the work of Mary O'Donohue. She was a post-producer for *The Oprah Winfrey Show* for over a decade, and as an author media coach, she helps authors get more media attention and maximize every minute. Connect with her at MaryOdonohue.com and tell her I sent you. While traditional media doesn't always result in a vast increase in book sales, you can use the logos, articles, or replays on your website to elevate your credibility. That third-party validation can make an enormous difference. I've noticed it because at least once a week someone will reference my TEDx talk or the article about *You Must Write a Book* in *Forbes* by Kevin Kruse.

- There's one more ideal team member, and they require their own section. There are some of you who might wonder a few paragraphs from now, why I'm suggesting helping other people market their books. It's pretty simple: many hands make light work, and helping many people means you'll have many people helping you.

Here we go:

Build Your Bench

Build your bench of author friends, that is. Develop long-term, mutually beneficial relationships with other authors, and you will not only succeed easier and faster, but you'll also enjoy every day that much more.

Why?

Other authors understand what you're trying to do; they speak a language only understood by other authors. Does your spouse or significant other (who isn't an author and might not even be a reader) want to talk about books, marketing, and developing other income streams, i.e., *work* all the time every day?

Nope. (Mine, either.)

Do your author buddies? Heck yes!

Other authors know what you need to know. Want to discover the best apps for writing? How to identify the best keywords and categories for your book? The best way to connect with a certain person on your list? Ask your author friends.

Other authors shorten all of your curves. Learning curves. Connection curves. Happiness curves.

My husband patiently sits through dinners with my mastermind author friends visiting from out of town and people I've met in my travels. He's a music and entertainment guy—bring up specific artists or bands, being on the road, or what it's like to run "back of the house," and he lights up like a Christmas tree. Book stuff the main table topic? Not so much.

I discovered my first real group of author friends at a conference in Austin, Texas, … seven (seven!) years after I published my first book. Being a self-published author, I had some worthiness issues, and it never occurred to me there might be other people like me. Please don't wait as long as I did to connect with other authors!

I'm here to tell you there are lots of people like you—and they want to talk about what you do (no matter your profession) and your book ad infinitum. You might not find them in the next office or cubicle over, but I promise there are many, and they'd love to know and support you.

On your to-do list, and soon in your MAP, is to develop a list of connections who are authors, both on your topic and many others.

Where you can find other authors you need to know:

- **On the bestseller list.** Writing a book on fertility? Look for fertility books on Amazon and in Barnes & Noble. Helping folks transition from a corporate career to being an entrepreneur? Focus on finding books by authors who have done just that.

- **Writer and author conferences.** There are big ones (e.g., 20Booksto50K, ThrillerFest, NINC) as well as little ones and virtual ones.

- **Bookstores.** Why not sign up for your local independent bookstore's email list of events and support the authors who come for signings?

- **Groups you belong to right now.** As a Rotarian and board member for Family & Children's Service, I'm in good company with a dozen other authors.

I'm sure you're wondering how to connect with them? I thought you'd never ask. Before you read this list, keep in mind that other authors are usually awesome, and they *know* (really know) what it's like out on the field. They will be more inclined to help you, discuss what's working for them, and provide encouragement than you might think right now. Trust me on this one!

- The first one is easy: When you meet an author, identify yourself as an author or soon-to-be author. You'll be friends faster than I typed this sentence.

- Buy and review their book—then email them about it.

- Or just email them. Dozens of times, I've connected with authors I admire and/or whose books I've read and enjoyed, and they've written back. Now we're friends. It takes time, but it's easy and also loads of fun.

- Follow them on social media. They might not recognize your name the first 10 times you like or comment on their posts. Keep showing up; I promise they are paying attention.

- Subscribe to their email list and respond to them with a comment, question, or encouragement.

These are just a few ideas. Eventually, you'll find yourselves in the same place, paths crossing, over a cup of great coffee, and Lord willing, a fine pastry will also be involved.

It just might be the beginning of a wonderful friendship. In fact, any or all of the above can and will be!

If you have a book, but you don't have a team and a bench, you can legit get started right now. *Today.* You won't have to guess about much because I've outlined the details (action steps to take) in your Matrix and your MAP. And it's finally time to dig into them and create yours.

Are you ready? I sure am!

CHAPTER FIVE

SUCCESSFUL AUTHORS HAVE BIG PLANS!

With a brilliant book, a solid team, and your creative juices flowing, you can put together a Book MAP that will destine your book for greatness!

CREATE YOUR MARKETING ACTION PLAN

In Chapter 1, I first talked about not leaving a book's success to chance. Over the years, I've created and refined the tools I'm sharing with you—the Book MAP and, in particular, the Matrix. While having *hope* is a must, it is not a book marketing strategy.

As a visual and strategic person, being able to craft my MAP and actually see it has been enormously helpful for not only putting it together, but keeping it top of mind (because I can print it out and refer to it often).

BOOK MARKETING MATRIX

To review, in your Matrix, there are four aspects: *Publish & Repurpose, Distribution, Promotion,* and *Selling.* (You'll find it in Chapter 2 if you need a visual reminder.)

Let's review these four important aspects of your book marketing, only this time going through each one.

Before I begin, I suggest you grab a legal pad, journal, or open a new Word document on your computer and capture the ideas you have for your book as I talk you through this. Also, put on your "I'm having fun" hat and enjoy this process—it is a blast!

PUBLISH & REPURPOSE

The first two, three, or four boxes in this first column are dedicated to the formats you intend to publish your book in.

First, I determine what formats I am going to publish the book in—usually always at least the e-book and the paperback. I suggest you, too, do at least these two formats.

I've been fortunate enough to have Rob Actis, the voice of *The Miracle Morning* book series, voice many of my books. I make sure he can do any book I'm working on and connect with him as early in the process as I can.

Audio is a fast-growing segment of publishing. More and more people are discovering audiobooks. They make it easy to "read" a book while working out, cleaning the house, or driving.

If you are expecting your book to generate clients, and those clients to pay a tony price for your services, you'd be well-served to publish in hardcover as well.

Once you are past those first three or four boxes, then you can use the remaining boxes to focus on how to repurpose the book's content into other formats and/or marketing efforts.

I *love* this part! I get to be creative, thinking about how my future readers will discover my work, and just maybe, I'll have the chance to connect and work with them.

I visualize them and imagine what they would like to have at their fingertips to put what I'm sharing into action. This lesson was brought to life the first time I got an email from a *Prosperity for Writers* reader. She said, *It sure would be nice to have a journal to do these exercises in. I've been using a notebook, but would you consider doing a journal?*

It's probably no surprise I immediately set upon creating the *Prosperity for Writers Productivity Journal.* And guess who got the first copy as a gift?

If you want to have a companion guide, planner, or journal to accompany your book, you'll dedicate a box to that.

If it makes sense to turn the book into a series, i.e., write more books on the topic from a different perspective or go deeper into a particular aspect of your topic, dedicate the appropriate number of boxes to that.

As you can see in my Matrix, I've only noted one additional book *(I Must Market MY Book Workbook)* to accompany this one.

In retrospect, it would have made complete sense to pencil out a series when I wrote *You Must Write a Book*, but hindsight is always 20/20, right?

Don't think that you'll magically be able to come up with all the ideas right away (but you just might!). Some of them (like this book) are a little tardy in showing up.

In this column, I also put ways I can repurpose the content for marketing. Such as declaring a National Book Marketing Month (March … I know, I know, me and alliteration), creating YouTube videos from reading excerpts or chapters, or putting together an initiative to turn this book into the gift you give a writer you love.

There's simply no right or wrong way to do it. It really just matters that *you do it.*

DISTRIBUTION

When you consider distribution channels, it makes sense to think about the best places readers can buy your book, as well as how they are going to consume it.

Global, National, or Local?

I helped Matt Feret create his book, *Prepare for Medicare.* It made sense to publish on Amazon U.S., as well as to enroll in KDP

Select (for subscribers to Kindle Unlimited—more on this later). Since Medicare is a program only for U.S. citizens, most of the focus for this book is the United States. However, we published worldwide as well.

Why worldwide? Because there are a lot of ex-pats living in other parts of the world who just may come home one day and need to know all about their Medicare benefits. Also, our military serves around the world, as do many folks working for U.S.-based companies. It only makes sense to have the book available from their current country's Amazon store when possible.

Another book I helped to create, and signed an NDA to work on (thus, no title or author name), was for a gentleman's business that provided services solely in his zip code. At $5,000 per month per client, on a five-year contract, each new engagement was worth $300,000. But he only serves businesses in his zip code and the surrounding three zip codes. The book we produced was short, about 15,000 words, small in dimension (4.2x7), and focused solely on his immediate geographic area.

Our marketing plan focused solely on him giving away his books and "training" his strategic partners on how and when to give the books away. I wrote about this concept in *Business Dating: Applying Relationship Rules in Business for Ultimate Success*, and I'll talk more about this in Chapter 9.

He buys the books 5,000 at a time and gives them away as fast as he can. Finally, he added the e-book to his website and email signature so anyone could have free access to it and would be automatically added to his email newsletter list (we talk about email in Chapter 6).

As of this writing, it's been six and a half years since we published his book, and he's sold *maybe* 1,000 copies (and only because some people insist on paying him for it). Here's the fun part: He's engaged at least 77 new clients directly from his book (no need to pull out your calculator; it has resulted in over $23 million in direct new business and much more in repeat and referral business). He's had to hire new staff and expand his office space (three times). He swears publishing a book is the second-best thing he's ever done for his business—the first best thing is continuously using it to market his business!

Does it make sense for your book to have worldwide distribution? Or does it make sense for you to focus on a smaller or specific geographic area? Do you want it in every big box and independent bookstore? Do you want to sell it on your own website, like Joanna Penn does with her books? (Check out www.CreativePennBooks. com.) Finally, should your strategic partners sell it or give it away?

That last question is getting into bulk sales territory, which is coming up soon. *Is there anything else you need to consider when it comes to distribution?*

PROMOTION

I view promotion (and selling) as the link(s) between publishing, distribution, and what I will do to connect my book with prospective readers.

Why? Because once columns one and two (Publish & Repurpose and Distribution) are in place, you won't need to fuss with them much. Your focus then becomes solely on taking the actions necessary to move the books into the hands and hearts of your readers.

> *"A book at rest is money at rest;*
> *a book in motion is money in motion."*
> ~Honorée Corder

You want your book to be *in motion.*

Promotion is yet another column with off-the-charts creative opportunities. There are now at least two fantastic places to advertise your books, AMS (Amazon Marketing Services) and BookBub. These both come with a steep learning curve and require a budget, patience, and consistency (and sometimes—well, many times—keeping up with changes and iterations).

There are probably opportunities for you to promote your book in industry journals or magazines, or even in publications ancillary to your work or even another area of interest.

If I played golf, I might consider running an advertising campaign in various golf magazines for *You Must Write a Book*. Golfers tend to be professionals who may, at some point in their life, want to write a book.

You can also advertise your book on social media, and we'll chat briefly about that later.

I'm a huge fan of guesting on podcasts, and I intend to launch one of my own soon, having been a guest on over 500 so far. If you love talking about your book's topic, podcast guesting can be a gateway to thousands, if not more, prospective readers.

Summits have become all the rage. I even hosted the Empire Builders Summit for the first time in 2021. I've been interviewed on a dozen or so as of this writing. It's a great way to put yourself in good company on a topic and get discovered by lots of new people all in the same week.

BookFunnel is my absolute favorite (and only) way to share my new books with an advanced reader team. It's also a fantastic way to join or host group promos to build your list. At the beginning of your author journey, join all of the promos that make sense. You can sign up to be notified when a new promo takes place. The downside is you have no control over who else signs up. (Sometimes, the other books in a promotion are by authors who can't or don't have the ability to promote much, so you won't see much traction.) Once you've found your footing, host your own promotion, and make it targeted by asking the other authors in your specific genre or area of expertise to join you. It makes marketing easier and more effective. Hosting a promotion with other specific authors and books is a way to engage the Also Boughts on online retailers, making it easier for the algorithms to organically market your book to prospective readers.

SELLING

Now you've made it to the sales channels, i.e., how, where, and sometimes, when will you actually sell your book?

Does it make sense to focus on one-to-one book sales or bulk? Or both?

You can see, in my column on Selling, my focus for this book revolves around getting in front of authors and aspiring authors. I filled my column with what makes sense for my book. You can use what I'm doing as a recipe for what you can do.

Since your book probably isn't a book about book marketing, let me share some additional options for, let's say, a book containing inspirational stories.

Pronounce "National Overcomers' Day" and discount your book on that day and over the weekend closest to the date. Invite people to share it with someone going through a rough time, such as a divorce, losing a loved one, dealing with a health challenge, or even someone who has recently lost their job. Stories of triumph are helpful and inspiring.

Craft a keynote presentation and give it to Rotary and Lions Clubs. The audience members will love you and your book and want to buy it on the spot.

You could sell your book in bulk to hospitals with people battling major health conditions like cancer or even people who have had "parts replacement" (think knees and hips). Perhaps you haven't thought to put your book in specialty or novelty stores in your small town (or neighborhood in your major city). There are usually at least a few in smaller towns and dozens in larger metropolises. I've found they are all very local author-friendly.

Since your book's message is universal, why not find a foreign rights agent or even reach out to foreign publishers to see whether they want your book in their language? No matter what language a person speaks, they need encouragement in their native tongue—and there's a publisher for that!

Another example—a book about preparing your own taxes for wage employees will sell a lot in the first quarter of the year (and for procrastinators in August and September to meet the October 15 extension deadline).

If you're a speaker, you'll want to sell your books in the back of the room after your speech. Maybe you'll sponsor conferences and events and have a booth where you sell books or even give them away.

I suggest always keeping a book or two (or five) on hand (and definitely a box in your car), and you can also sell those books when the opportunity presents itself. What you'll want to consider here is what you want *more*: Do you want to gift the book to someone who is a prospective client or simply sell it? What you do in each situation will depend upon your ultimate desired outcome.

Because I have an entire ecosystem surrounding almost every book I've published, I lean toward gifting a book when I have the chance. I'd rather have someone buy the companion planner, take the course, or even hire me to coach them or speak to their group than pocket twenty dollars.

Book sales might be your focus, and bulk sales might provide a tremendous opportunity for you. Bulk sales have, in some years, been as much as 20% of my total income. The retail profit is high, and once you've got the systems in place, processing them can be an easy, lucrative, and fast way to earn revenue.

A bulk sale can be as few as 10 books or even 100,000 or more. The sky is the limit! With print-on-demand through Amazon or IngramSpark, you collect the money, and they print and ship the books. You can even use an independent printer with the same process.

THE MATRIX IS JUST THE BEGINNING!

Why do I share all of this? Again, this is about helping you to learn how to think creatively about book marketing. I want you to have a window into how I think about book marketing for each book I write—so you can mentally place your book in different scenarios to design *the one* that will work perfectly for it! I also want you to be empowered to think creatively about your book marketing because creative thinking is what will keep the books in motion and new clients in motion toward you and your business.

Once you've completed your Matrix, grab a fresh cup of tea or a cocktail and do a hair flip! You've got one of the major components of successful book marketing in … well, the books!

Next, we'll tackle the rest of your Book Marketing Action Plan. Once you have *that* done, your book's success is all but assured!

BOOK MARKETING ACTION PLAN

Your Book Marketing Action Plan (your "MAP") is straightforward; however, it consists of more than a half-dozen elements.

The entire plan is over 15 pages. You can see my full example for this book and a blank example to create one for your book in the *I Must Market My Book Workbook.*

Following are the individual components and how I think about them when plotting out my MAP:

Book Marketing-in-Action. This section defines your time and financial commitments to the book. I answer two seemingly simple questions:

1. How much time (daily/weekly) will you dedicate to book marketing?

2. How much money is available for book marketing?

I say "seemingly" because your book *is an additional time and money expense,* on top of everything else you're already doing.

For this discussion, I'm assuming you're not independently wealthy, being carried around on a pillow all day while a large group of minions carries out your menial everyday tasks, thus leaving you with unlimited hours to market your book endlessly.

Note: If this is you, we need to talk. I kinda wanna know how you did it.

I digress.

I am also then assuming you have a full-time job or own your own business, have friends and family you want to see and be seen by, and have the usual financial commitments, making you both time prudent and fiscally aware.

With that in mind, you'll want to think about the two questions like this:

1. Do I have time every day to complete one or more of the actions on my MAP (such as writing a newsletter, posting on social media, being interviewed on a podcast, or creating an episode of my own)? If so, how much time do I have, and when is that time? Or do I need to batch my action items into one day—and on that day, how much time do I have?

2. How much money do I have to dedicate to my book marketing?

I left the money question hanging for a reason: you won't know how much money you might need or want or will even be able to estimate for another several pages.

The reason is while it takes *some* money to market one's book, the amount of your investment can vary significantly. It can range from being scrappy (giving away digital books via BookFunnel at the cost of $100–$150 per year) to spending a more substantial sum, where you give away $10 hardcover copies with dust jackets, regularly mailing them to probable purchasers far and wide.

You may have no budget for advertising, or you may allocate as much as $100 a day to Facebook, BookBub, or AMS.

I treat each book as its own little business, with my company "loaning" the book what it needs until it makes money. I'm usually in the red at around $10,000 by the time I launch my book, so I keep my marketing budget in line until I'm in the black.

Because I look at each book as its own business, under the umbrella of my bigger businesses, I know the book will return my investment almost immediately, especially with the right MAP.

Before you put together your budget, allow me to briefly re-share my earlier example:

I published *I Must Write MY Book Workbook* shortly after publishing *You Must Write a Book*. Requests for a course led me to launch what is now Publishing Ph.D., Building a Million Dollar Book Business, and the Empire Builders Mastermind. This book, the companion workbook, and the course Book Marketing Mastery joined this business and are all under one umbrella—the bigger umbrella of my larger company.

Now I did not map this out from the beginning—I wish I had! It wouldn't have taken me six years to get these assets in place.

What I lacked in future planning, I made up for in "following the breadcrumbs:" I paid attention to the reviews, the responses to my emails, the unsolicited messages and emails, and what people were asking about. Readers wanted more information on *how to write a book*; this led me to create the course. They wanted *a place to capture their ideas, track their timeline, and note their progress*—this led me to do the workbook. When I spoke at conferences, I talked about the Wheel of Fortune, otherwise known as "ways to repurpose your content and create other income streams." That led me to create Building a Million Dollar Book Business. Finally, I mentioned starting a mastermind to someone who said, "If you have one, I'll join!" The Empire Builders Mastermind is now in its fifth year, and I plan to go for at least another five. My only regret is I didn't think to start it sooner!

My hindsight and experience can now be your foresight.

So, you can see why those two little questions aren't so little in the overall scheme of things. While I invest several thousand dollars in my books, you can see why that's a literal drop in the bucket for the returns I see.

Suggestion: Complete your MAP and then come back and answer those questions a second time with your broader view. That's what I do.

BOOK MARKETING PRE-LAUNCH PLAN

This book is about book marketing, so I'm working under the assumption that you have already launched your book. Before I continue, allow me to explain why I don't go into detail about your book's pre-launch plan here.

Some of you might be upset about the fact that I have a whole philosophy about putting together a book pre-launch, and it is not included in this book. I do hope you're not disappointed if this book is your first exposure to me. Don't fret, I've got you covered with some resources to help you.

I cover my philosophy on book pre-launch, *a little because it is so complex,* in *You Must Write a Book* (which you can get for free at HonoreeCorder.com), and in much more detail in Publishing Ph.D. When you sign up for this book's bonuses, you will also find a coupon to use for $500 off of the course.

While book marketing is the focus of this book, book marketing (as I mentioned) does begin the minute you begin writing the book and continues in the launch of the book. I do suggest checking out the course for a 360-degree view of every little detail.

It makes sense to set goals for your book, and I set goals for each book, which inform and influence how much/often and to what extent I'm marketing the book.

As you have already launched your book, I still recommend you take the time to set some goals for the next 90 days (or one year). Executing these activities is excellent for getting new eyes on your book (regardless of how long ago it was published). While you can't necessarily get the exact same amount of traction for a longtime published book as you can with a brand-new book, you can certainly breathe new life into your enthusiasm as well as reignite interest by keeping at least a modicum of focus on the book's marketing.

As an example, here are my goals for this book:

- Goal #1: 15 reviews by Launch Day, 3.5 stars or higher (average)
- Goal #2: 100 reviews (by March 23, 2023)
- Goal #3: 500 podcast interviews.

In the MAP example in the book bonuses, you'll see there is a bit more to this page.

BOOK MARKETING DURING LAUNCH DAYS 1-30

Starting on the official launch day of the book, I focus on two goals for the first 30 days:

1. What is my daily sales goal?
2. What are my daily actions going to be?

Experience has taught me that eventually I'm going to tire of doing multiple activities for the book, not to mention the fact that I often run out of time to make it a major focus due to my other responsibilities. This may happen to you as well.

But for those first 30 days, I'm prepared to be out of balance, knowing the launch period will soon be over. Also, what I'm going to be able to do in the subsequent months and years for the book will pale in comparison to this first 30 days. During this first month, I am laser-focused on the results I want to get in terms of book sales and what I'm willing to do to get those results.

Allow me to interject a little "woo woo" into our conversation and encourage you to set, and track, a daily sales goal. Write it down every morning in the form of a gratitude-focused affirmation:

I am so happy and grateful to sell 50 books today!

You might even go so far as to continue with something like:

My book is really gaining traction, getting reviews every day, and making the impact I've always imagined it would make.

It's no secret to those who have read my other books that I'm a big believer in helping things happen by writing them down. If you're new, please just trust me on this one. The results will surprise you.

Back at "AsYouPrayMoveYourFeet.com," I'm also a firm believer that you must take consistent, intentional, and persistent action to also encourage those results along.

To that end, I select seven action items to do (or have done by me and my assistant) every day. The seven comes from my conversation with Jack Canfield—he and Mark Victor Hansen did seven things every day to get *Chicken Soup for the Soul* to become the best-selling trade paperback series of all time in 2008.

Revisit your time and money commitments in the Book Marketing-in-Action section. This will guide you to the actions that will be most time and money effective. You don't have to do seven. You can do five, or three, or one. Before you decide, look back at your goals and make sure your actions are congruent with your goals.

One last thought—I did mention that sometimes we have a block of time on one day to focus on our book marketing activities. I love to work in time blocks and batches, so I do this as well. Scheduling tools are your friend in this case—using tools that pre-schedule posts, sending newsletters that are pre-scheduled, and putting interviews and other media all on the same day (obviously when possible) will allow you to "set it and forget it."

BOOK MARKETING DAY 31–FOREVER

Just when you've got your sea legs about you, you'll wake up and, just like that, the first month will be over! You'll probably be tired and also pretty psyched about being an author with some great results to show for your efforts.

You'll notice that for this book, and all of my books, this page is very similar to the previous page and my action items.

You'll also notice the word *forever*. That's because your book is not (again) an avocado—it doesn't go bad! Unless you have time-sensitive content, you can sell your book *forever*.

Again here, you'll want to consider the amount of time and money you have at your disposal and how much of each you're willing to devote to your book.

If your book does what you want it to do—this is where I'm going to assume you want it to generate new clients and business—and you find it is working, you'll want to stick with whatever action items are working (more on analyzing them later).

BOOK MARKETING ACTION ITEM CHECKLIST

This section of the MAP is where I make my master list of action items—the ones, first identified in my Matrix—that I want to do on a daily or weekly basis.

The thing I focus most intensely on is engagement—the social media platforms I've chosen to engage with, my email list, readers who leave reviews, and other authors and experts.

Ultimately, any action I do comes down to whether what I'm doing is moving the needle on book sales and building relationships. Even if the tactic is what "everyone else" is doing (and it might even be working amazingly well for them), if it doesn't resonate with me and/or it doesn't work for me, I remove it from my checklist.

What you see on my current checklist for this book is a list of action items that have worked like a charm *for me* with past books. Keep in mind, they've also worked great for other authors, and they might work great for you, too! (I hope they do!) But if you see something on the list, like "webinars," and you have a visceral response to them, *don't do them.*

Study the master list of possibilities (you can even do some additional research and identify some different ones), choose the ones you like and think will work for you and your book, and go to town putting them into practice.

When you're finished with that, it's time to ponder your network.

CONNECTIONS: YOUR NETWORK IS YOUR NET WORTH

The next several pages of your MAP consist of your connections. A couple of questions to prime your pump of creativity:

- Who do you know who needs your book?
- Who do you know who serves those who need your book?

You may have several categories; there's no right or wrong number here. Obviously, the more categories you have, the more opportunity you have. Having said *that*, the more categories you have, the more people you need to connect with, and therefore the more work you'll have to do to connect effectively with everyone in those categories.

For this book, I'm keeping it fairly simple (at least to start). Here are my categories; you can use them or define some new ones of your own:

Clients/Customers who would benefit from the book. For my business, this includes students of my other courses, current and previous mastermind members, and those on my newsletter list (authors and aspiring authors).

On your list, include all of your current and past clients, and co-workers who serve the same demographic. Really anyone you have already served with your knowledge and expertise could be a good person to talk about your book to others.

Industry professionals. I know lots of folks in the book business, including people who serve authors (editors, graphic designers, ghostwriters, copywriters, agents, publishers, etc. (just to name a few!)). They are all going on my list.

Who are the professionals who do what you do and serve who you serve? If they don't have a book (and even if they do), their audience, followers, or clients would benefit from your book. Doesn't it make sense to share their book with your audience (it does), as well as find a way for them to share your book with their audience? Books and book marketing simply are not a zero-sum game.

I'll switch gears away from the book business for a second and use a traditional business example. A business attorney serves businesses (stay with me here, that eye roll wasn't necessary), as do CPAs, bankers, commercial real estate brokers, insurance providers, and financial advisors (and there are many others).

Who serves the same folks you do? Make a list of the different categories of professionals, then make a list of each of the people you already know in those categories.

Strategic Partners. Similar to, but not exactly the same as, industry professionals. These people serve the same people you serve but are not in competition with you and *are likely to collaborate with you* (or they already are). This list can also have the names of people who do *not* serve your exact ideal reader or client, but they are awesome, and you can collaborate and cross-promote.

Similar to the industry professionals above, make a list of names. Hang on; I'll give you some action steps shortly.

Other authors—just like you! These are the folks who have authored books on the same or similar topics as yours. They are the same folks you really should know, and they really should know you—or at least know *of* you, as well as perceive you as a legit person in the same space.

As I mentioned earlier in this chapter, having author connections is fantastic! I admired many of my now author friends for a long time before we became actual friends. And don't worry; I'm going to share exactly what I recommend you do to develop those relationships.

Pretty happy with your list? Great! Now, here is what you can do with and for each one of them (and you'll note it is very similar to building your bench of author connections):

- Look them up online. Sign up for their email newsletters on their website. Respond to their newsletters with a positive thought, some encouragement, or a question. *Get on their radar in an awesome way!*

- Connect with them on LinkedIn. Professionals tend to have a profile there, even if they aren't all that active. Follow them on Instagram, Facebook, and Twitter—any or all of them if you are on those platforms.

- Order a book they've written, or two, or three. *What? They've written on your topic? Great! Include a quote or passage in your book (I promise they'll love it!).*

- Once you've read the books, write reviews for them on the platform where you purchased the book, and put it on Goodreads as well for good measure.

- After you've made a connection, offer to send them a copy of your book. *If you mentioned them in your book, just send them the book. Be sure to mark the page where you mention them, sign the book, and include a note inside the book as well as a handwritten note to accompany it.*

- It will make sense, eventually, to offer to jump on a Zoom (you could send them a link to get on your schedule), or even meet for coffee. I've had great coffee, lunch, and dinner meetings with people who live close to me—or we've gotten together when we've been close enough through our travels to connect. Yes, this is time intensive, and absolutely worth it. *There's nothing like face-to-face time to deepen and strengthen a relationship.*

- This one might be the most important of all: Share about them and their book(s) where it makes sense for you to do so. Recommend their book to your email list and social media following. Interview them on your podcast, and ask them to interview you on their podcast (and make sure to share the interview and say nice things about them and their book while you're doing the interview).

Before you reach out to someone, consider the relationship you already have—do you already have a good relationship and rapport with them? Or do you need to work on the relationship first before you ask them to help you market your book?

As an aside, very few things are more irritating than hearing from someone only when they need something (can I get an Amen?), so please don't reach out to people *solely* to ask them to buy your book or help you promote it. This is a list of people you already have a solid (or at least budding) professional or friendly relationship with (or would really like to!) and who would be happy to hear from you now.

As a final note on this section, and as I've mentioned previously, I have an entire book on this topic: *Business Dating*. It is a complete road map to developing long-term, win-win, mutually beneficial relationships (if you're into that sort of thing). Success in book marketing (and in life) doesn't happen in a vacuum. It happens because it is created on purpose, and having a wonderful group of people on your bench and in your corner makes success even sweeter.

SOCIAL MEDIA

The Social Media portion of your Book MAP is next.

If social media isn't your jam, *you do not have to do it.* In fact, I've included this section in this book, but it is nowhere to be found in my Book MAP. Why? Because social media is, for me, pure fun. I don't use it for business very often, although I do at the request of some of my business partners and clients, on occasion.

Many authors swear by their Instagram posts, their TikTok videos, or their consistent posting on LinkedIn (I'm the last category). But I've worked with several authors personally who have almost zero social media presence, save a LinkedIn profile that is sparse, and their book sales are just fine, thank you very much.

Because social media is constantly changing, this section, while it could be long and detailed, is going to be brief. As a smart, ambitious author, I will hold you capable of identifying, studying, and mastering the social media platform of your preference, with a couple of small suggestions:

- Keep it simple … Don't overthink what you're doing. There's no need for a complex social media schedule or posting plan. People like authenticity, great information, and bonus points if you're funny.

- … and short. By short, I mean "in the amount of time you spend." I can open my phone to check Instagram for "one minute" and three hours later still be looking at it. Not really, but I have spent a lot of time I could have put to better use on social media.

- Get your advice from a terrific expert. The only platform I focus on using for book marketing and client development is LinkedIn, and my expert of choice is Brynne Tillman, who is the "LinkedIn Whisperer" and CEO of Social Sales Link. She has a course (or two) to maximize one's LinkedIn effectiveness and she is a master. She's one of those people who I wish would keep talking when I listen and learn from her. Find out more and connect with her on LinkedIn here: www.linkedin.com/in/brynnetillman.

BUILDING WORD OF MOUTH—YOUR "GROUND GAME"

You've probably heard me say, "The number one way a book and/or author is discovered is through personal recommendation. Word of mouth is second to none."

Your "Ground Game" is a combination of your social interactions and the media you appear on. Not "social media" in the way we just talked about it, though.

SOCIAL

The social in this conversation refers to the real, in-person connections you have or have had in the past. Think of your high school friends, college buddies, or co-workers from previous jobs. These social connections could be close to home or even in places you used to live—I still have strong networks in Honolulu, Las Vegas, Austin, Dallas, and NYC because I've stayed in touch with people there over these past 30+ years.

Please note: I do not advocate launching a book and asking "everyone" to buy it. My scientific, proven method for a successful pre-launch and launch is shared in exact detail in Publishing Ph.D. If you want to ensure you engage online retailer algorithms for long-term organic sales, you'll want to check that out. End of commercial, but I would be remiss if I didn't clarify this up front.

Now, here are just a few bullet points to jog your memory:

- **Local and long-distance personal friends.** Who is in your backyard, and who used to be? *Your friends will want to help you market your book!* My bestie took copies of *The Miracle Morning for Teachers* to schools in her town. In fact, as social-emotional learning, and support tools, they can help students everywhere, and she's not the only friend who is helping.

- **Local and long-distance professional connections.** This list may have some crossover with a previous list in your plan. Thinking of someone twice more than doubles the fact you need to reach out to them. *smile*

- **Philanthropy and giving back.** Do you serve on a board or volunteer for any organizations? If so, chances are you've made some great connections there.

- **Spiritual or religious connections.** Those who worship alongside you can be wonderful, supportive connections.

- **Hobbies, special interests, or affinity groups.** My hobbies are fitness, Feng Shui, and French (and eventually learning other foreign languages). I've connected with people around the world, not in the spirit of business at all, and ended up finding readers and clients. You can, too.

- **Neighbors—yes, your actual neighbors.** It is easy to underestimate the power of knowing your "neighbors," i.e., having connections where you live, even though the majority of your business is worldwide (as mine is). You just never know what magic might result from introducing yourself (and maybe your book(s)) to your neighbors.

- **But wait, there's more!** I'm sure there's a category of folks you interact with regularly that I am not thinking of—but you are. Add them to your list!

Now that you've got (most likely) *pages and pages* of names, here's what you can do:

- **Provide an email** (such as the one at the end of the Book MAP example) **to them and ask them to send it to 5 or 10 people they think might be interested.** Think about it—if you have 50 people on your list, and you probably have many more than that, and they each tell five people, that's 250 new people that are getting a direct recommendation to check out you and your book. Cool, right?

- **Buy a box of 100 books** (if that's in your budget) **and give them away.** Close friends and family members will want one. You're a famous author now, and those closest to you will want bragging rights.

- **Always have books with you when you go to social, club, and professional meetings.** I set an intention to find the perfect person to give a book to, and that part is always fun.

- **Send out your own email and ask who would like a copy— to have and/or to share.** You'll be surprised who is excited to receive and pass on your book.

- **Repeat after me:** *"Books at rest are money at rest. Books in motion are money in motion—and I keep my books in motion!"* Then get your books in motion.

MEDIA

I have yet to meet anyone who has said, "I turned on the *TODAY* show to find my next book to read."

Having said that, being featured in traditional media can be likened to boarding the express train to your desired destination. Being featured in "newer" forms of media, such as podcasts or blogs, can also be a catalyst for connecting you with readers.

As I said previously, both provide terrific third-party validation.

I've had my share of traditional and non-traditional media, and they have all served to build my brand and bring new readers and business to my door (or inbox).

I have words of caution surrounding *getting* on traditional media, and even being featured on some podcasts. The fact is that they can cost a pretty penny. Even if you make multiple seven figures a year, I do not recommend you throw money at a PR firm for placement on traditional media without thoroughly thinking it through. PR firms can cost thousands or even tens of thousands of dollars *per month*. You must sell a lot of books in order to earn book royalties to even cover those costs.

If you are using your book to engage new business, even a substantial investment in getting into the media could be a rounding error. I just want to make sure you're carefully considering all sides of the equation before you move forward.

There are a few things you can do to keep costs in line and maximize your reach:

- **Hire an author media coach.** Previously mentioned, she deserves another shout-out here: Mary O'Donohue is a former post-producer on *The Oprah Winfrey Show*, and she provides a thoughtful process for not only identifying the right media, but also making the best use of it from all angles. With her course or some one-on-one consulting, you'll be on your way in no time.

- **Be a podcast guest.** Aim to pitch more than five podcasts a week (until they start pitching you!), with the goal of being on one or two podcasts a week. Your ultimate goal, in my experience, is 500 podcasts. It might take you five years to appear on 500 podcasts, but there is a quiet momentum that takes over, and you'll love what it does for the consistency of your book marketing efforts and sales.

- **Guest post on blogs.** I still get requests from people who want to provide guest posts. I don't accept them or provide them, but lots of people do. If doing some free writing is okay with you, identifying a blog with the reach of your ideal reader, I say go for it!

THE REST OF THE MAP

The final pages of your MAP consist of miscellaneous yet effective pieces of your book marketing efforts. In brief, they are

- Seeding the market. Since my first book, I have "planted" my book in places where I hoped the perfect person would find it. I've left it in doctors' offices, on airplanes, and in coffee shops. I've even gone rogue and left it in bookstores with the intention that the bookstore would sell it and order more to take its place. (It totally works, by the way, although now you can get bookstore distribution by publishing through IngramSpark and asking the bookstore to order a copy to have on the shelf.)

- A social media post for friends and family to use.

- An email your connections can use to help get the word out about the book.

- A list of podcasts you want to appear on.

All right, we've covered a lot. You've read a lot to understand *how* your book's marketing can come together and perhaps even completed the first draft of your plan. Take a break, and when you're ready to tackle email list-building and learn about some tools that will make your life easier, turn the page.

CHAPTER SIX

TOOLS & OTHER BOOK MARKETING NECESSITIES

Every very successful author I know has a tool belt, and in that tool belt, there are several things that have contributed to their success:

1. An email list
2. At least one tool to help them write better and faster
3. A website
4. Their preferred writing software
5. Coffee *smile*

For those of you who looked at the first one and cringed a little, I have many words of assurance.

EMAIL LIST-BUILDING AND MAXIMIZING

Let's start with why building an email list is important in the first place. After all, there is a school of thought that social media is the best place to connect with readers and potential readers. Right?

I'm not going to dispute the beauty of social media *for some authors*; however, unless you are the founder of a social media site, *you do not have a way to contact your followers if something happens to that site.*

Read that again. It's important. I'll wait.

Okay, I understand you might have 300,000 people in your private Facebook group. You don't? Neither do I. But hold on a second.

What happens when your identity has been hacked, your group is shut down for violating an ever-changing posting policy, or the algorithms shift in favor of paid advertising? If you haven't moved those folks over to your email list, the number of followers you have won't matter.

That aside, *engagement* is what matters for both social media and email lists. But I'm getting ahead of myself.

So, I'll say it again (and this isn't to make those of you who have exactly seven people on your email list panic, it is to encourage you to act now), *the only thing you own is your email list.*

Your job is growing it. Nurturing it. Curating it. Culling it when necessary.

My friend Tim Grahl, author of a book I highly recommend, *Your First 1000 Copies*, talks a lot about email lists and authors, and the importance of authors having their own lists. In fact, he has worked with dozens of authors with books on the *New York Times* lists—and his number one strategy is helping them to grow their email list.

I remember Tim speaking to my Empire Builders Mastermind a few years ago. He told them to ask themselves two questions every day:

- What can I do today to build my email list?
- Is what I'm doing building my email list?

Again, you're smart, so I don't have to keep on this point for much longer. Suffice it to say the best time to start building your email list was 10 or even 20 years ago. If you haven't focused on it or even started, the next best day to start is *today*. So, shall we?

STARTING AND GROWING YOUR LIST

If you have yet to start building an email list, this section is for you. (If you've already got tens of thousands of names on your list, skip to the next part.)

Find a provider. The first thing you'll need is an email list provider—one with a great reputation that is considered "friendly" by email services. If you just send lots of emails from your inbox (my strategy the first few years before I knew better), your emails will end up in spam, which of course, defeats the purpose of sending the email.

There are dozens of providers. As of this writing, I use ConvertKit after years of using AWeber. There is also Mailchimp, Keap, Kartra, and many, many more.

Two things to consider here:

- **Think long-term.** You see, I switched from one to another? Hello, gigantic headache. Sign up with a provider that will allow you to grow. I recommend you not go with a free service; you'll have to switch at some point! You'll have to pay in the beginning, but it isn't a lot—and your book is meant to generate new business. You'll be able to write it off, and it will work hard for you.

- **Figure out the functionalities you need today and over the long term.** You'll probably want landing pages, the ability to create multiple lists with the email sequences that go with them, and maybe more.

Don't overthink this too much (or at all). Do your research, pick one, and start using it.

All of the top email service providers have incredible training, so block out some time on your calendar and learn the basics. Send out your first email, even if it is to just seven people. *Everyone* started out with just a few people, even those with millions on their list today.

Define your topic(s). Your next decision is to determine a theme or area of focus for your newsletter. Hint: It should be on the same topic(s) as your book; really, the main work you're doing. I write books about writing books and all of the surrounding topics. My books are specifically about the art and science of self-publishing, and my topics range from how to craft a book from the blank page to marketing and turning book topics into multiple income streams.

Guess what? That's what my newsletter is about, too. There is a lot of ground for me to cover, and in the six years I've been sending a newsletter, I've covered a good bit of it.

Even if your book is about a narrower topic, there are most likely dozens of angles you can take when writing your newsletter.

I have a hint that might be helpful:

Use a monthly theme. Break down your content into twelve sub-topic areas. Then, list the months and assign one of your sub-topics to each month. Depending upon your newsletter schedule, which I talk about next, you could simply use an excerpt from the book each month. Or if you're sending twice a month or even four times a month, you could dive deeper into an aspect of your topic that wasn't covered in your book.

Nail down your schedule. Decide on your email sending schedule and stick to it. Whether you decide to send multiple emails a day (don't do that, you're not J.Crew!) or just one, two, or four emails a month, commit and stick to your schedule. Your subscribers will come to expect to hear from you—they like it; they opted in, remember. And they want your email!

A FEW POINTERS:

- **Only add people to your list with their permission.** I love some of the emails I get that I signed up to receive—other times, I'll start receiving someone's email "magically" after we've met. If you think someone would be interested in your emails, forward them the latest edition, and say, *I think you might find my regular newsletter interesting. There's a link to subscribe at the bottom, or you can reply, and I'll manually add you. You'll need to confirm your subscription either way, and you can unsubscribe at any time.*

- **Make sure to use the "double opt-in."** Meaning, they sign up and then confirm their sign-up. Even then, you'll have people unsubscribe later because they've forgotten they signed up. This cracks me up, but it does happen. I'm sure I've done that, too.

- **Provide great information and a little something personal, too.** As I mentioned, author buddies are the best—some of them were "my friend" (in my mind) long before we actually got acquainted because I read their emails. Jeff Goins is terrific at sending valuable insights and ideas, along with what's going on with him personally. Your subscribers want to hear from a human being, not a human doing. Share the best stuff you've got about your area of expertise, and also let them know your favorite kind of chocolate (dark), what you do in your free time, and even the story of how you wrote your book.

MAKE THE MOST OF YOUR EMAIL LIST

I am not an email marketing guru—there are so many. Ben Settle is an excellent resource for perfecting the art of writing emails, specifically copywriting. He will even teach you how to sell to your list. Bryan Harris, Shane Sams, and Grant Baldwin all share great copywriting tips, tools, and ideas.

I'll defer to those guys on the finer points of email marketing, and I suggest you pencil in some time to study it. Owning something—your email list—is one thing. Knowing how to make the most of it is another thing entirely. I study it regularly and always pay attention to what I like and don't like about the emails I receive.

In my years of sending emails, almost two decades now, I've learned a few things, so here are two strategies that have worked for me that you might not learn from others.

WHAT TO WRITE ABOUT ...

As I suggested above, break down your main topic. For me, it's "writing, publishing, and monetizing books."

For writing, I talk about how to write, when to write, where to write, why writing a book is important, the benefits of writing a book, strategies for writing faster, writing when time is of the essence, and the list goes on.

For your list, think about the problems or opportunities your reader has, and list them. Then take a deep dive, one email at a time, into each facet of your topic.

I backed into this strategy by creating too much content, deciding to analyze it to see whether I could reuse it without alienating or upsetting my readers, and maybe even streamline my process.

For example: With *The Successful Single Mom* books, I wrote a blog for years. For quite some time, I wrote daily. Eventually, I had trouble coming up with new and interesting ways to write about any particular aspect. In addition, I felt like I'd written all of the books on the topic I wanted to write. I was also remarried and had moved on from the single mom phase of my life, and I wondered what I could or should do next.

It occurred to me it might make sense to evaluate all of my content and see whether there was a way to continue to help single moms while alleviating my need to constantly create new content or put so much focus on that piece of my business.

DO AN ANALYSIS—EVEN BEFORE YOU START!

In my analysis, I made a list of sub-topics related to becoming, being, and navigating the challenging life of a single mom with grace, poise, and ease. Since there were six books in the series, I immediately had six main topics:

- Becoming a single mom, dealing with the shock, and getting adjusted
- Cooking meals and snacks
- Finding new love
- Getting fit
- Becoming financially independent
- Going back to school

Then, I focused on identifying blogs I'd already written and put them under the sub-topic that fit the best. Finally, I looked at the data of the blogs—which ones were the most popular and had the most comments and shares? If I were doing this today, I'd notice which newsletters got the most traction or how many unsolicited replies I received. Since I also post these newsletters on LinkedIn, I look at those posts to see what's resonating. This is important later.

If you've had a blog or newsletter for a while, you might have this kind of data at your fingertips. However, if you're just getting started, you might not have any data yet. For now, just go with your gut (i.e., do what makes sense), and you can do this type of analysis later to see whether you need to delete, expand, or rewrite some of your content.

Some of you might not like my advice to "go with your gut." But here's the truth: You know the answer because you're writing non-fiction. This is your area of expertise, and I believe in you! I'm confident that if you think it through, you'll know the right answers.

Once you've got your main high-level topics, brainstorm the next level. In other words, go deeper into a topic. Highlight the sub-topics that seem to have the most juice. Managing one's divorce means getting the emotional support you need, learning how to co-parent, and identifying what you can do with yourself when your kids are with the other parent.

THE LIFE CYCLE OF A READER

Once you have your list, think about the life cycle of a client or customer.

When you're considering creating content for a newsletter, you don't have to commit to writing new content *forever*. You can pay attention to the life cycle of your subscriber, and once you've cycled through all of the logical content you have to share, start sharing it from the beginning.

Over the years of writing the single mom blog and hearing from readers, I noticed a general trend: the life cycle of a single mom, from divorce or break-up to getting remarried or being in a committed relationship, is about three years (36 months).

I paid attention to my unsubscribes and the messages that accompanied them: *It's not you—it's me! I'm happy to say I'm unsubscribing because I am getting remarried in a couple of months, and I don't need to read about being a single mom anymore.*

Thirty-six months of a life cycle, with two blogs a month, meant I needed to identify the 72 most popular blogs, focusing on the most popular posts on a certain topic. Single moms are busy, so I figured a cadence of two blogs a month would be enough to help them, and not too much that they'd unsubscribe from having too much information too fast.

From the publishing perspective, I've noticed it takes someone about two years once they get on my list to tell me they've published their book. I've never written about what to do after you've gotten remarried (although, as of this writing, my second and final very happy marriage is going strong at fourteen years) because I don't get those questions. I am writing this book about marketing because I get questions about book marketing just about every single day. Every podcast I'm a guest on, and just about every email I get asking a question that isn't about publishing, is about marketing.

Over this past summer, I did a book marketing series, and I got dozens of emails daily thanking me for helping with that aspect of being an author. As it turns out, it doesn't matter whether you're an indie (self-published), hybrid, or traditionally published author—you want to know how to sell more books. I took my own advice and am following the breadcrumbs—providing additional books and products to serve what my market is asking for.

Because I wanted to automate my content and move onto a different focus, I did my analysis in reverse. I suggest you do yours … today!

Of course, the blog is there if they want to do what I like to do—read all the things about a topic I'm interested in, by an author I'm fascinated by. Of course, along the way, I recommend the book or books on the topic I've written and those by other single mom authors and bloggers I think they should know.

PUTTING IT ALL TOGETHER: STRATEGIZING YOUR EMAIL NEWSLETTER + CONTENT CREATION *FOR* BOOK MARKETING

When I'm thinking about content now as I work on new areas of interest, I try to do all that I did with my single mom books and blog *before* I launch a newsletter and work on a new book.

HERE'S YOUR EXERCISE:

- How long is a client likely to engage with you (i.e., identify their life cycle)?
- How often should they receive your newsletter?
- Do some math. For this example, let's say you'll have a client for five years, and they should get an email newsletter from you twice a week. That's roughly eight times a month for 60 months, or 480 newsletters.

Before you shoot the messenger, me, consider the fact that you could probably recycle the same information every year or even two. I mean, I recycle my newsletters with lightly updated information—and I've never had anyone say, I can't believe you resent the same email in 2018, 2020, and again in 2022! If I hear anything, it's: "Thanks for the reminder; I needed to hear that (again)!"

Your 480 newsletters might only be 96 or 192 (which is still a lot, but keep in mind you create the content the first go-around one at a time). I wrote over 700 newsletters for the single mom blog, and I wrote them one day, one post at a time, for several years.

I look back and can only imagine how much time I could have saved if I had known and used this strategy back then. You're welcome. LOL

Now that you have a handle on your email newsletter, which I consider (and I hope you do now, too) a central part of your book marketing, we can flow nicely into the other tools, applications, and resources that will make book marketing a more efficient effort on your part.

BOOK MARKETING TOOLS, APPLICATIONS & RESOURCES

There are so *many* wonderful platforms, apps, tools, and other resources you can use to share about and sell your book.

My role here is to share the ones I know and use or have used to some success.

Two things to keep in mind: There are others I hear are great that I don't use (I mention a couple of those here as well), and *you don't have to use any or all of them*. I'm sharing what I use, why, and how. There might be something even better for you, or you may not want to execute a particular strategy. Book marketing, as you now know, requires a certain level of strategy, and the list below can help you execute that strategy effectively.

I hope I'm encouraging you to think differently than you might have in other situations where you've looked to an expert for insight and information. Take everything I say with "a grain of salt" and run it through your own "do I want to do/use that?" filter. I like to keep things simple, so while it seems like I'm using a lot of different things to market my books, in truth, I'm keeping it to the minimum effective dose to get the greatest possible results.

These are listed in alphabetical order, not in order of preference.

Anchor. Anchor is a podcast app I first learned about from Stephanie Bond (she's amazing, look her up—and read more about one of her book marketing strategies in Chapter 8: Distribution, Sales & Selling). It's a free app that takes a lot of pain out of creating and launching a podcast. While writing this, I'm finally planning to release *The Honorée Corder Show* in the next quarter (you'll have to check and see whether I haven't gotten to it on my list yet). I feel encouraged that I can do it because my colleague Lucas Marino (training business expert) is using Anchor and swears, "It's easy!" I've chosen the name, and I'm working on getting a graphic made, all while plotting what topics and threads I want to explore on the show. If you're reticent to start a podcast, I say give it another thought.

BookBub. BookBub is a kingmaker—get a featured daily deal, and your book could sell thousands, if not tens of thousands of copies, on the day it's featured, and the lag effect could have enough juice to keep your sales going for weeks, months, or even forever. I remember swallowing hard and paying over $800 for my first BookBub back in 2012, hoping I would at least break even. Well, I more than doubled my money back in that one day (you have to sell a lot of books at Amazon's 35% royalty rate to make $800), and the sales continued for quite some time.

Since the early days, I've had several other deals, and they've continued to add more options for authors to engage with prospective readers, including personal book recommendations, creating an author page others can follow, and even producing ads.

BookFunnel. BookFunnel is how I distribute my book files to my Advanced Reader Team, for free on my website and through my email signature, and in other creative ways. It is a way to share those files without creating the opportunity for the theft of your IP (intellectual property). I borrowed this straight from its website: *"The essential tool for your author business. Whether it's delivering your reader magnet, sending out advanced copies of your book, handing out ebooks at a conference, or fulfilling your digital sales to readers,*

BookFunnel does it all. Just like you, we're in the business of making readers happy. Let us help you build your author career, no matter where you are in your journey."

You can integrate BookFunnel with your email service, which builds your email list (and we're all on the same page about the importance of that now, yes?) while sharing your book. It works like a charm on both fronts.

I happen to know the creator of BookFunnel and was at a conference when he floated the concept. I've been using it from Day One, and it is, without question, one of the best investments I've made in my author business.

Dropbox. Many folks use other applications for storing documents and even working collaboratively with co-authors, but my hands-down choice is Dropbox. Why? Because you retain all ownership of rights. Other platforms—and don't just trust me on this, read their fine print—can exercise ownership over documents you create—including your spreadsheets, manuscripts, and, yes, even what you put in an email.

Rev. Rev is a fantastic app if you want to dictate your content and have it transcribed easily, for a reasonable fee, and PDQ! Several ghostwriters I know use it to write their books, and I'm using it to crank out blog posts and other content (including a fun book project I'll get to finally publish in late 2023). You can even do interviews and identify who's speaking when you upload the file. The transcript will come back to you with about 98% accuracy. Considering how much faster people generally talk than type, it's a brilliant way to get words out of our heads and on paper.

Slack. Slack is a terrific way to communicate with co-workers or even groups of people on a platform that is free or not very expensive—it also isn't a social media platform that could go down or lock you out at any moment. I use Slack with my team, as well as with my mastermind. (I also use it in foreign language learning, and in a couple of instances, with writers' groups that have formed after conferences.) Slack is similar to Facebook, in that there is a main channel to read, and you can also join smaller channels (like Facebook groups) for special interests or smaller group conversations. You can even send private messages between people.

It has recently added a voice messaging option, which is great. I love that I can share files, pictures, and information, but it isn't public ... so unless someone is invited and approved, they can't just show up and do what they want.

Trello. I'm super new to Trello, as of this writing, but it is all the rage with highly productive people I admire—Lucas Marino, as mentioned earlier, with Marino Training, and J. T. Ellison, a world-famous fiction author. Both of them have *excitedly* shared how Trello keeps them on top of multiple projects, and in my short time in the saddle, I concur with their enthusiasm.

Voxer. I use this voice message service with business partners and even one of my mastermind members who lives in the United Kingdom (so we can't voice text).

Voice texting should probably get its own mention, so here it is—it is great to get a fun voice message from someone. Can we agree? While tone and context can get lost in writing (you can't tell I'm deliriously happy while I'm writing this, can you?), listening to someone's voice can almost leave no doubt about how they feel about something. You can use Voxer on any type of phone, so if you're an iPhone user but some of your friends aren't, you can still send them a voice message and include photos, videos, memes, or even files.

WordPress. WordPress is the gold standard for websites and is fairly easy to work with to launch and optimize a website. A basic template doesn't cost much, and even a computer neophyte can (if they want to) put up a site, make changes, and even add a plug-in or two. If what I just said is Greek to you, or you simply don't want to do it, WordPress is also affordable when engaging a website designer. It will allow you to add pages and create different and expanded functionality over time.

A FEW OUTLIERS

Following are a few apps that aren't directly related to book marketing, per se, but they sure do make my life easier and, therefore, my book marketing easier and more effective. They might seem out of place in a book-on-book marketing but trust me on these—they might enhance your life and make you an even better book marketer.

Evernote. I use Evernote for *so many things* related to book marketing. The plans I shared in earlier chapters? I put copies of mine in there, in case I need to reference them on any digital device (e.g., iPhone, laptop, or iPad). Want an easy place to be able to review receipts for book marketing expenses or see the list of other authors and their books? Evernote is fantastic for these and so much more.

Pandora. Music makes everything better, and Pandora is a free music app that allows you to listen to music pretty much non-stop (and definitely non-stop if you pay a low monthly fee). I have different playlists for different endeavors, and while you might think that due to my ability to market and sell books, I just loooooove doing it, there is some slogging-type work involved. I get through my book marketing to-do list with some great tunes.

Pzizz. Pzizz is a nap, sleep, and focus app. I mostly use it to take "nappuccinos": a 25-minute nap preceded by a cup of coffee or even a Vivarin. (Don't judge, caffeine is a hack that helps me buzz through the afternoon just like I slept until 8 a.m.!)

ThinkUp. If you discovered my work through *The Miracle Morning* book series, then you're probably an affirmation practitioner. This app allows you to write and record your affirmations in your own voice, and then play them back to you. Want to be a more confident book marketer? (Yes, you do.) Then get the app and record this affirmation: *I am an effective book marketer! I focus on book marketing, and every day, more readers discover my book(s).*

It's super fun to see your words come to life right before your very eyes.

That's it for apps. If I think of others, I'll be sure to add them to my website: HonoreeCorder.com/Resources. Check back regularly for other cool book writing, publishing, and marketing tools I discover and love.

A final word on using most "free technology": *don't.* When something is free, that means you're both the product and at the will of the person or entity that does own it. Which means, again, that at any moment you could be locked out of or lose what you've created entirely.

I learned this from my very techie husband: As soon as you can, purchase your own servers and either pay a team of people to handle the particulars, or learn how to do it on your own. We own our Enterprise email software, servers, and firewall, and locate them at a data center that only we (and our small team) have access to. Although they are quite expensive, I happily pay for them. You might wonder why, when there are ample free or low-cost options available. The answer is simple: Unless there's a literal power grid failure, my email and website work. No one can turn them off or shut them down.

One last thought: If you do use platforms like LinkedIn, for example, be sure to download your contacts into an Excel spreadsheet once a month or so as a backup.

I hope by now you've got the beginnings of a very solid plan and are feeling confident about putting the building blocks in place for a long and happy book marketing effort and many happy returns.

But we're far from done. There's quite a bit more for me to share so you have a complete picture. Let's get into timelines and analyzing your results along the way.

CHAPTER SEVEN

TODAY, TOMORROW & THE FUTURE

With everything I've introduced to you thus far, I'm sure you've figured out book marketing isn't finite—it simply doesn't come to an end. Marketing your book is a long-term endeavor, and when you combine your goals, enthusiasm, and the things that work, you're much more likely to succeed.

This is worth repeating one (I promise) last time:

Your book isn't an avocado—it won't go "bad" (unless it is a specific type of book like *Your 2020 Guide to Job Seeking*).

Your book can be as valuable, and perhaps invaluable, a decade or two from now to readers as it is today. To help it make the biggest impact, I suggest having short-, medium-, and long-term goals and a plan to back them up.

You've got the plan, so let's dive a little deeper. There are three distinct phases to a book's marketing life, starting with the beginning when the book and everything about it is exciting and new. This begins in about the first six months and lasts up to a year. Make the most of that energy when you're still full of vim and vigor about your book! We're going to talk about how.

Then you get into Phase Two, which typically lasts into the second year. In this phase, you're still learning what puts your book in the hands of readers, and what that can do for you and your business.

Finally, when your book isn't so new anymore, it will still have great bones and unlimited potential. Think about how *Think and Grow Rich* is still selling after many decades, and consider how your book just might do just as well!

This time period then is, not surprisingly, Phase Three. Phrase Three has two or three options: You can move into maintenance marketing, where you keep enough of your own focus and attention on the book to keep it connecting with new readers—or you can double down on your marketing efforts. You can engage in even more promotion and marketing, create a companion product or alternate source of income, write another new book, or all three!

PHASE ONE: LOVE AT FIRST SIGHT

Your Shiny New Book

In the beginning, when you're a new author, you say with massive enthusiasm, "I've got a new book!"

After about six months or a year, the newness starts to wear off. Your book is just like a great relationship.

Don't believe me? Remember the last time you were in a new relationship? You thought you'd never stop going out every night and getting away a couple of times a month. You'd stay up all night chatting, and then live on adrenaline at work the next day.

Eventually, you find your rhythm and settle into a routine. Daily date nights turn into weekly date nights and weekends away evolve into a quarterly or twice-a-year vacation.

Over the long term, you know that to "keep the love alive," you have to spend quality time together, but hey! You've got responsibilities! You've got work to do, the kids have a zillion activities, and throw in an aging parent or two, and voilà! You have to do the things that really make a difference, while still juggling everything else that needs your attention.

If you're still in the "I'm a new author! I've got a new book!" phase, I say embrace it and enjoy it while it lasts. You're going to sacrifice giving your attention to other obligations and commitments, and rightly so.

Getting your new book the proper launch and boost it needs now will make a difference later. (If your book has been out for a while, go on ahead and skip to the following section that applies to you.)

You're in this phase if your book hasn't yet launched or you've launched it in the past 6 to 12 months.

It's important to have short-term book marketing strategies: i.e., you've got a great book, and you market it tomorrow by getting on two podcasts this week. Podcasts *love* having authors on to talk about their new books. Independent bookstores are thrilled to have signings for new releases. Book clubs, publishers, and online book supporters (like Goodreads) are consistently looking for new books authors with great energy, and they love to promote newer titles.

One of the reasons I advocate for a January release over a September–December release is because, within a few months, your book is "last year's book."

Once your Book Marketing Action Plan is complete, highlight, mark, or notate the short-term action items that are time-sensitive, ones that are crucial to focus on right now. In this beginning phase for new books, I focus on doing those three to seven action items per day. I check my sales several times a day, reply to every review that's left for me, and the list goes on.

REAL-LIFE CASE STUDY: NEW AUTHOR BETH ANN RAMOS

One author in Phase One of her book is Beth Ann Ramos, founder of Good Day Books and author of a children's book, *I'm Getting New Glasses!* A former corporate marketer, Beth gets frustrated when she sees businesses spend money on unbranded and disposable promotional products, especially those aimed at children. Each time her kids are gifted an unbranded goody bag, she laments the business's missed marketing opportunity. She can't wait to throw those random trinkets in the trash. What a waste!

With this in mind, Beth set out to create a promotional product that helps kids and serves businesses well.

I'm Getting New Glasses! tells the story of Olive, a little girl who is nervous about getting her first pair of eyeglasses. With the help of her little brother, Andy, they begin trying on new frames. Together, they discover that getting new glasses helps you see clearly and can also be fun.

Beth used her marketing background and InDesign knowledge to learn Illustrator and bring her character sketches to life. Beth's husband is an optometrist and her biggest fan. So, when her book was finished, she created a custom version for his office with a fully branded full-color ad on the back cover. Her husband appreciates having an effective marketing tool for his practice. Beth is having a blast encouraging and connecting with young readers and their parents.

(We'll pick up on Beth's story in Chapter 8).

In the meantime, learn more about Beth at BethAnnRamos.com.

It is so fun to have a new book!

This is the phase where you can really help your new book become a staple read and even gain momentum week over week and month over month. Focus on the now, and the immediate future, while keeping an eye on what's coming up next.

Which brings us to ...

PHASE TWO: YOU'RE STILL THE ONE

Staying True to Your Book

In traditional book circles, your new book quickly loses the attention and focus of your publisher (and any assistance they've been giving it via their PR firm or connections). Frankly, new books are coming out all the time, and they want to keep 'em coming.

Note: This is not even a little bit critical; it is simply a fact. The publisher's job is in their title—to publish books. Without new books being published, they don't stay in business.

However, this is the reason we've been inherently taught to move on to the next book. Either a book swims or sinks within the first 12 weeks of its traditionally published life. If it swims, it continues to get attention. If it doesn't, there are hundreds of others in the queue that might.

But your book, *your book*, regardless of who published it, can and dare I say, should get your loving, caring, and consistent attention from Day One. No, actually from months before Day One (official launch day). Forget the publisher, if it isn't you, of course, and focus on your book. And now that it's been out for a while, chances are *everyone* has tired of it (at least a little), but this, my friend, is the time to downshift—to find a brand-new gear that allows you to continue to love on your book and keep the momentum you so intentionally had for it in Phase One.

Let's say your book came out in September of 2022, and now it's March of 2023. Last year's fall release is this year's spring must-read. Good job! You've got dozens or perhaps hundreds of reviews, and you've really engaged the algorithms. But you're getting shorter on time because your book is doing some of the heavy lifting, and your calendar is filling up.

Mid-term book marketing encompasses the next 6 to 12 months of your book's life and consists of a portion of the action items you used to get your book selling—the ones that really moved the needle.

Using my previous advice about analyzing the amount of time you have, along with other resources, to focus on marketing, now is the time to identify one to three things you can do daily or weekly, consistently, over the next six months to a year.

If you're on a daily schedule and only have five minutes, post a quote from your book on LinkedIn. Take a snapshot of a great review and share it on Instagram. Or send out three postcards to prospective clients.

If you're limited to a small window of time for weekly book marketing, try choosing three effective strategies from Phase One. For example:

You could: 1. Send out your twice-monthly newsletter, 2. Do a poll on LinkedIn, and 3. Be a guest on a podcast.

Or 1. Speak at a conference, 2. Make five calls to encourage bulk sales of your book, and 3. Attend a conference and be a sponsor.

REAL-LIFE CASE STUDY: AUTHOR ANDY STORCH

Andy Storch is the author of *Own Your Career Own Your Life* and a speaker and trainer. He specializes in helping professionals create successful, fulfilling careers and also helps companies retain their best employees. Andy does this through speaking, training, holding live events, and hosting a membership community.

He's squarely in the middle of Phase Two of his book marketing efforts, most notably because two major events occurred as Andy was writing and publishing his book. First, the COVID-19 pandemic effectively shut his business down and limited his speaking and training engagements. Then Andy was diagnosed with testicular cancer, which spread to his stomach and neck and forced him to stop working for a few months.

While the cancer treatments made some marketing efforts (like podcast interviews) challenging, Andy was still determined to take regular action and build his business. After all, cancer is expensive, and he had big goals of building a business and brand around his book.

While Andy faced many challenges, it took a while for the seeds to bear fruit. His efforts paid off, though, with multiple paid keynotes for global companies, and a major software company booking a rollout of his training program that is based on his book. Recently a client even flew him business class from the U.S. to Berlin to give a keynote presentation to all of their employees to teach them to own their careers.

Andy sent me a series of text messages, even as I was writing this book:

> *I know you know this, but it is so fun to have a book! Especially when you are traveling and talking to people. So, fun!*

> *I am flying back today from Berlin. A client flew me over there and paid me a bunch of money to give a keynote about my book. So good!! This was the dream! This was the plan!*

> *And everyone I talk to is so excited about the book and the topic. I was just in the airport lounge in Newark talking to this couple, and they were so excited when I gave them a copy. So, fun!*

Yes, Andy, it is so fun! He had one more text in response to my thought about why it was working:

Yes. I followed your process, and it took a while, but I have seen great results!

Andy is a shining star of an example of how having a solid marketing plan and working that plan consistently, even in the face of major obstacles, can work.

In fact, this middle phase can be so powerful that once you get a couple of years into your book's life, you can, with a little effort, continue to see better and better results.

PHASE THREE: TOGETHER TILL THE END OF TIME

Marketing from Here until Eternity

By your book's second or even third birthday, the bloom can be off the rose. You're no longer a new author, and your book is no longer a new book.

But if you think I'm throwing in the towel on your business's second greatest asset (second only to you, my friend), you are sadly mistaken.

Just like anything that's two or three years old, the fun is just getting started, and the best can be yet to come!

If you've already sold one million books, congratulations! (If you haven't, there's still plenty of time.) But even if that's the case, with *eight billion* people on the planet, your work to find every possible reader for your book is far from done.

You can market it—until you release the next book (but there's some important fine print associated with this!), until you retire, until you change professions entirely, or until you leave this Earth.

My vote is (a) for the final option and (b) that it be a long, long time from now.

The fine print on "releasing the next book" is that *this* is actually one of the more effective ways of selling your current book. We'll talk about that later, though.

For now, let's stick to what long-term, consistent, persistent, and (most importantly) effective book marketing looks like.

This book's predecessor, *You Must Write a Book*, is six years old as of this writing. Over these past six years, I've consistently focused on selling it and have sold it, with the direct, indirect, and bulk numbers topping 70,000 copies in all formats. In addition, I've given away more than 500 physical copies (and counting), and over 6,000 digital copies through my website, email signature, and countless other promotions.

In my next book, *You Must Monetize Your Book* (which will be followed by *You Must Build an Empire*), I'll talk about how far and wide you can go with a book, featuring *You Must Write a Book* and several others. (Be sure to stay in the know by grabbing a spot on my email list: HonoreeCorder.com/ReviewCrew.)

Why am I still hocking *You Must Write a Book* after six years? Great question—so glad you asked!

That original book, in what will eventually be a full series of three main books and three companion workbooks, is accompanied by *I Must Write My Book Workbook* (you'll not be surprised there is also *I Must Market My Book Workbook*); a course, Publishing Ph.D. (yup, you probably know about the companion course for this book, Book Marketing Mastery, by now, don't you?); a third course, Building a Million Dollar Book Business (the companion book will be *You Must Monetize Your Book*); and (my very favorite), the Empire Builders Mastermind.

I've been hired to help publish a little less than two dozen custom books because my clients read my book and thought hiring me would be the best and fastest path to becoming an author.

One thing has led to another, and the brand is still continuing to expand under what I now affectionately refer to as the "You Must Umbrella."

This book, the series, and the additional income streams are enough of a reason (cough) to keep marketing my book. *When you're thinking about your book's long-term marketing, think about where the book could lead the reader—both in terms of doing business with you, and in the transformation they will experience by coming into contact with you, your book, and your work.*

There are a lot of reasons you can find to keep marketing your book long-term, but as we've discussed, you might think the sun is setting on your enthusiasm for pouring tons of time into it.

This is where the rubber meets the road, and you decide how you will spend your time and money over the foreseeable future when it comes to your book.

Keep in mind there have been almost six years between publishing *You Must Write a Book* and commencing work on *You Must Market Your Book*.

For these past several years, I've focused on marketing *You Must Write a Book*, and I've been strategic with my time. I've kept my total book marketing time to less than three hours per week, save when I have a podcast interview that takes up an entire hour by itself. Three whole hours might sound like a lot, but those 12 hours a month are the basis for a nice percentage of my total income. I consider them inviolate and worth their weight in gold.

I'm sure you read over those past few pages and thought: *Why didn't she do the series, journals, and courses in order?*

Another great question. (You are so smart!) The truth is, I didn't do what I'm suggesting you do: take a step back and look one, five, or ten years down the road and envision the entire empire as built, and then set forth on the journey of building it.

I did something that also works, something I also suggest you do: follow the breadcrumbs. I didn't have a clear vision for a *You Must* series, courses, and mastermind in place when I started. I was just writing one book for one event! Rather than overthinking it or beating myself up about it, I've just continued to expand it one day, one book, and one offering at a time.

One could argue either one is the better route; the truth is, the one that's the best is the one that works for you. Sure, I've probably left money on the table—maybe lots of it. But I'm not overwhelmed with an unending list of things to do, unwritten books, and unrecorded videos for courses. I'm happily building one step at a time.

Now that you're up to date with how creating the You Must Umbrella has strategically helped grow my business, I'm going to share what I know works for me, based on my experience with the book in its Phases One and Two:

- **Interviews.** Mostly podcasts, but I was fortunate enough to appear on episode 40 of Pat Flynn's SPI TV, "Book Publishing Tips with Honorée Corder," in Kevin Kruse's Medium article "Why You Must Write a Book (And How to Do It"), and I even did a "Fishbowl," an internal Amazon interview that is broadcast around the world to Amazon employees. There have been many others. You can find many of them at HonoreeCorder.com/Media.

- **Content.** You might know about this book because you read my LinkedIn newsletter or are on my email list. I regularly share the best I've got in bite-sized pieces, through collaborations (hey, *Miracle Morning* peeps!) and online summits (hi, Summit watchers!).

- **Good, old-fashioned in-person networking.** I'm a longtime Rotarian (RotaryInternational.org), and in my club, I'm known as the "book lady." I serve on the Family & Children's Service Board of Directors. I'm a member of Jen Gitomer's Your Success Frequency Membership group and I attend at least one in-person or online networking event (strategically chosen … hey, I'm an introvert, remember?) every month.

I cannot stress enough how important human connection is for marketing your book and how it factors into personal recommendations—as we know, personal recommendations are *the number one way people discover books.*

With podcast listenership growing daily by leaps and bounds, and the fact that people immediately do an internet search when they want to find great information, I know from looking at the data that those first two bullets provide a continuous stream of readers to my books (and other offerings).

Also, as the entire process of writing books is incredibly personal, I have found some of my best clients because I've met them in person, or I've met the person who referred me to them in person.

As someone who probably wouldn't ever leave home if I didn't have to, I know I must leave home in order to make those connections—and I also recognize that I must allow myself time to recharge. In order to get what I want, I have to get outside of my comfort zone on occasion. You might have to, as well. If I don't take those risks, I won't get the commensurate rewards.

It's your turn to think through what your long-term and most effective book marketing action items could be once you're in this stage.

My last thought on this is that it's never too early or too late to discover a tactic that is a game changer. You could have published your book years ago and implemented one or two ideas that exponentially increased your sales.

If I ever discover something that would work better than what I've been doing, you can bet I'm going to innovate the heck out of my plan! I encourage you to courageously do the same. By all means, strive to keep it fresh and interesting, never get bored, and even enjoy the process.

It could just be that someday your grandkids will be marketing your book and putting themselves through college!

Let's shift gears and talk about the different options for selling your books.

CHAPTER EIGHT

DISTRIBUTION, SALES & SELLING

The distribution channels you choose (or have chosen) for your book can impact its success over time—both in sales and fulfilling the roles you've assigned to it. Along with distribution, the opportunities to sell and market your book are vast and require you to have the insight needed to make the best decisions for you and your book. Allow me to provide an overview and an amount of insight that can help you round out your marketing decisions.

There are several excellent distribution channels available, and just in case you've yet to publish your book (or you've published it and are wondering what to do in the future), they are included here.

DISTRIBUTION

For the longest time, indie authors were light on choices when it came to book distribution. Well, no longer! Thanks to Amazon, IngramSpark, Kobo Writing Life, and Draft2Digital (to name a few), self-published authors have the exact same distribution channels as traditionally published authors.

Your book, regardless of the publisher, can be purchased wherever books are sold—around the world and in your local independent bookstore.

If your book has been traditionally published, your book should be available everywhere. If and when you receive your rights back on those books, you will have the opportunity to republish your book on those same channels. If you have self-published your book, your limitations are now so small as not to be noticed (with one exception, as of this writing: foreign rights—but this is not without possibility as well).

The moral of this ever-evolving story is that the sky is the limit; you get to choose. Isn't that wonderful?

DISTRIBUTION STRATEGY

As with all book marketing, strategy is involved in how and where you choose to publish, which will affect your choices and results.

AMAZON EXCLUSIVITY OR GOING "WIDE FOR THE WIN?"

Before I weigh in on whether your book should be sold solely on Amazon or published everywhere, let me explain the difference.

Also, it's not for me to decide what you *should* or *should not* do, but to give you some insight, perspective, and options so you can make an informed choice.

Amazon has a program, KDP Select, that allows authors a few incentives:

- You get a boost for your sales as a brand-new author when you first publish.

- Readers enrolled in Kindle Unlimited can read your book "for free," and as the author, you get paid for the page reads. The per-page royalty varies. You can learn more at KDP.Amazon. com (at the bottom of the page, you'll find a few links to learn more about the KDP Select Global Fund, KDP Select, and Kindle Unlimited).

You enroll for 90 days at a time, and by enrolling, you solemnly swear (legally) that you won't sell your e-book anywhere else during your enrollment period. Also, you can automatically renew your enrollment or stay in the program for 90 days at a time for as long as you like.

In fact, Amazon exclusivity is a great debate among self-published authors. If your book is traditionally published, your publisher may get your book the perks of exclusivity while still publishing your book wide.

Publishing wide simply means you publish your book everywhere you can (or want to).

"But Honorée, what should I do?" I know, you just want me to tell you, but I can't. Here is my perspective from my experience:

- Amazon does sell the lion's share of books. That's the truth and a fact. I probably buy one thing on Amazon about every other day, definitely a few times a week. Most people have become reliant on Amazon for good prices and ease of delivery, and this includes books. Many authors, even those who don't choose exclusivity, report that the majority of their income is derived from their Amazon royalties. I owe a big thanks to Amazon during my career—I got my start publishing on Amazon in 2004. *However.*

  Unless you are Jeff Bezos, *you do not own Amazon.* The old saying "Put all of your eggs in one basket and watch that basket" could apply here. If your basket can be taken away at a moment's notice, or you can't access your basket, therein lies the problem.

  There are authors who have had significant problems with, and because of, Amazon. I won't take up space talking about them here; I just want you to have your eyes wide open if you choose exclusivity.

  Amazon exclusivity is a fine choice if you are limited in the amount of time you have to market your book. One place to send people, also the one they are probably already visiting every day. To end on a positive note, you can get traction with the algorithms and sell more and more books over time and earn a significant amount of money. Amazon's marketing machine is finely tuned and can reach more readers on your behalf in thirty seconds than you could reach in thirty days.

• Publishing your books on *all* (or many) of the available platforms for sure gives you the most control. It also requires more work.

There are incredible publishing platforms, Kobo and Draft2Digital, to name just two, created by and for authors. They do an amazing job at being author-friendly, continuing to iterate and optimize for their authors, and providing distribution to the four corners of the earth. Joanna Penn talks about this on her podcast, *The Creative Penn*, and on her blog. Publishing wide is a good idea if you have more time than not to market your books. It is also good if you don't have any geographic limitations—i.e., the "what else" you offer isn't limited to a specific zip code, state, country, or region.

I *generally* recommend Amazon exclusivity for the first 90 days to first-time authors. This is to engage the algorithms to get the biggest and best launch possible. But my clients are busy professionals who don't have time to manage multiple platforms or the budget to advertise everywhere. Your situation may be entirely different.

You definitely don't want to choose exclusivity if you want to hit a bestseller list (think *New York Times* or *Wall Street Journal*) because they have channel sales requirements (you have to sell so many books through several channels, and Amazon alone doesn't check those boxes). There's also some tiny but important print here that matters, and it is best explained by Tim Grahl in his article "The Truth About *The New York Times* and *Wall Street Journal* Bestseller Lists," which you can find here:

https://booklaunch.com/the-truth-about-the-new-york-times-and-wall-street-journal-bestseller-lists/.

Your distribution strategy comes down to your short-term and long-term outcomes.

OTHER COOL BOOK MARKETING IDEAS

Just as your distribution strategy will affect your book sales, there are countless creative ways to sell more books—and some of them will be for an incredibly high profit margin!

1. **BookTok,** the book side of TikTok, has almost made Colleen Hoover a household name. You probably remember just a few short pages ago, I said TikTok is not for me. But that doesn't mean it's not for you! If putting together short, fun, or informative videos is your jam, BookTok might also bring more readers into your universe.

2. **"Free gift" with purchase**—a free download of worksheets, a limited-edition coffee mug, or even an online course (valued anywhere from $5 to many hundreds of dollars) can entice readers to buy.

3. **Another gift option.** Let's take the above one step further— very often, institutions, including schools, don't have a training or speaking budget, but they do have a book budget. Offer a free training or presentation, even an online course, to go with a bulk book order. I created a staff and teacher training to go with *The Miracle Morning for Teachers.* I offer it on the bulk sales page of my website and provide one enrollment for each of the books purchased in a bulk order.

4. **Guest blog posts.** While I'm not one of them, many bloggers love having guest posts to share with their audience. Do a search for folks who write in or around your area of knowledge, and offer to provide a post with a short byline mentioning your book.

5. **Quora.** You can become an expert who answers questions on this site. I've connected with hundreds of folks over the years, and I don't focus too much on it (I can imagine it could be even more effective if I did). I only answer questions that are in my lane and leave the rest for someone else.

6. **Book clubs.** There are local and online book clubs, and readers *love* authors! You can connect with the host, the group can read your book, then you can come and do a teaching, entertain a Q&A session—or both!

7. **Readings.** Corporate book clubs are also becoming more popular. I spoke at Cisco in 2018 in Northern California. There were about 30 people in the room, but the company broadcast it all around the world to every office. I did the same thing at Amazon in 2016, where they called it a Fishbowl. *That* was super cool!

8. **Book trailer.** I've seen a lot of cool book trailers in my time—they aren't cheap to produce (if you pay someone), but if you have a film student in your midst or you've got a 4K camera lying around and find fussing with some editing software a breeze, you can create a fun trailer. With video being all the rage, a video about your book can be fun and effective.

9. **Craft fairs, farmers' markets, and community centers.** Anywhere there's a gathering of creative people, writers are welcome. Take a couple of dozen of your books and hang out with some other locals, all while meeting prospective readers.

10. **Grocery stores.** They sell books at grocery stores; why not yours? It's a total bonus that while someone is picking up dinner ingredients, they can meet you and buy a copy of your book.

11. **"Gyms."** Gyms are in quotes because I want you to consider your demographics—you'd offer to have a book table at your local gym(s) if your book is about nutrition, health, fitness, or any related topic. If you have a money book (e.g., management,

investing, or debt), you could hang out at a local bank, sign and sell books, and meet prospective clients.

12. **Gift shops, car washes, and gift shops in car washes.** There are independent gift shops (there are several located right on Main Street in downtown Franklin, Tennessee, that I love), gift shops in museums and tourist attractions, and even in our local car wash (there was one where I lived in Austin, too). *All of them sell books!* Your book can be in there, ready to be discovered while someone is (a) visiting from out of town, (b) looking for the perfect gift, and (c) while they have a little time to spare.

13. **Podcasts.** I've talked about podcasts before, but not in this way. Stephanie Bond, a prolific mystery, romance, and romantic mystery writer, writes some of her books in serial format. I've long been a fan of Stephanie's and was delighted to meet her after she spoke at a writer's conference in 2021. There I learned about her series *Coma Girl*. I could write an entire chapter about her serial and the ways she's repurposed that content. But here's your takeaway: She developed a podcast that reads the daily episodes of her serial, one short episode at a time. Why couldn't you read your book in podcast format, providing another free way for prospective clients to listen to it?

Honorable mentions go to trade shows, conferences, and local clubs, including book clubs, special interest clubs, and even sports and golf clubs.

Now, let's turn our attention to one of my favorite ways to sell books: bulk book sales (and I've even got a bulk book special option you might love)!

SELLING BULK & CUSTOM BULK BOOKS

Why sell one when you can sell tens of thousands? I got my first taste of the awesomeness of bulk book selling when I published my first book.

By asking, *Would you like to buy between 10 and 100 books?* and then, increasing those numbers to 100 and 1,000, respectively, I was able to make bulk book sales right out of the chute.

Don't get me wrong; I enjoy selling one book to one person— every reader matters—but selling in bulk is not only fun, but the results are also great, too!

It was *Chicken Soup for the Soul* co-creator Mark Victor Hansen who put the idea in my head to make those asks. Ultimately his idea has led to many of the books I've sold in bulk.

Why is this such a great idea? So many reasons, but this one is my favorite, and it's a two-in-one!

Increasing your single effort, while simultaneously focusing on a bulk sale, multiplies profits and saves time.

You've heard the phrase "many hands make light work." Well, this idea works in reverse, too. Just a few bulk book sales can move many books. One conversation can lead to a bulk sale of 50, 100, or even 10,000 books, multiplying your profit by 50, 100, or even 10,000 times. It also doesn't take *much more* time to make a bulk sale than a single sale. Selling 10,000 books might take an hour of time total (okay, maybe three), but I guarantee you it is impossible to sell 10,000 single books (in the same fashion) in less than 30 hours! Your profit margin is higher because you pay less when you buy in bulk.

When considering whether your book is a prime candidate for bulk sales, ask yourself these questions:

- Could other professionals like me use my book to promote their businesses? *i.e., does it make the case for why hiring someone in our area of expertise is a great idea?*

- Or could those professionals use your book to help their clients problem-solve? *i.e., does your book help their clients or customers have a better experience, even as they provide their expert advice?*

- Could companies, groups, or associations use my book as a resource, textbook, or something else? *i.e., book clubs within corporations have become commonplace; sales managers or teams sometimes have suggested reading lists and will buy a copy for everyone in their group.*

If the answer is yes to any or all of them, it's probably time to add *bulk book sales* to your list of things to do!

If you're not sure, allow me to share some examples in the same order as above:

- Business coaches have used my books *Vision to Reality* and *Business Dating* in their coaching practices. The former makes the case for engaging and utilizing coaches; the latter provides a process coaches can help their clients implement for expediting success through intentional networking and relationship development.

- *If Divorce is a Game, These are the Rules* is used by divorce attorneys to help their clients navigate their divorces. They encourage them to adhere to a code of conduct and engage the services of others who would help (think therapists, physical trainers, etc.), all while allowing the attorney to focus on the legal side of their divorce.

- *The Miracle Morning for Teachers* and several other books in the series have become social-emotional resource support tools for teachers, administrators, and even full school districts. They provide a positive process that allows teachers and students to manage stress and get better results.

None of the above books were written with those outcomes in mind, but they've all sold successfully and continue to sell, nevertheless.

Idea: imagine writing a book *for the specific purpose* of bulk sales *because* the book solves problems or provides solutions for buyers and readers alike.

ONE STEP FURTHER

Sometimes selling in bulk isn't enough; sometimes, the buyer wants the books to be customized.

The idea of custom bulk book sales was given to me by a bulk buyer—he simply asked if I would mind putting his company's information on the back cover, so he wouldn't have to risk his business card getting separated from the books.

He was already buying in bulk, directly from Amazon, when he asked for a meeting. He even offered to buy the minimum number of books *of my choosing (!)*, so I'd allow him to customize it.

I agreed to back cover customization only and required him to buy 1,000 books with a setup fee. [Note: If you want my exact road map to facilitate a bulk book order, check out my course Building a Million Dollar Book Business, and get $1,000 off with the coupon code MKTGBOOK.]

He has gone on to buy 10,000 copies of the book every couple of years or so, and it isn't surprising he's the number one guy in his field in his state (the only reason he isn't a national success is because he's geographically limited by his profession).

REAL-LIFE CASE STUDY: BETH ANN RAMOS, AUTHOR OF *I'M GETTING NEW GLASSES!*

You'll remember Beth Ann Ramos, the author of *I'm Getting New Glasses!*, who I first talked about in Chapter 7. She wrote her book to help promote her husband's optometry practice and to help kids feel great about getting new eyeglasses.

Let's face it—if you got glasses as a kid, it might not have been the best experience in the world—perhaps you were teased by the other kids or felt like you needed them because something was wrong with you. I digress.

Within two months of publishing her book, and as of this writing, Beth has become a trusted vendor for a national group of independent optometrists and is providing bulk purchase opportunities to eye doctors nationwide.

Kids love reading this book (every copy I have personally loaned out so far is not being returned). I'm told Beth's husband loves it because it is a practical marketing piece that is far more effective than some of the others he's used, and it is helping kids to feel confident about wearing glasses.

This is a triple win! Oh wait, let's not forget the fourth win! It's a huge win for Beth, too, because she's making book royalties, bulk book sales, and custom bulk book sales.

Beth's story is a great example of how creativity can help sell both singles and multiples of your book. But your book can also help grow your business—exponentially—and it's fun!

Okay, you ask, how can it possibly do that? Please read on, my friend.

CHAPTER NINE

MARKETING *WITH* YOUR BOOK

Because some of the main reasons you've written your book are to increase visibility, engage more business, and make more money, you can use your book as your main business marketing tool.

There are numerous ways to market with your book, so let me share my favorite (and, dare I say, most effective) strategy: marketing your business with your book.

BEST "MARKETING *WITH* MY BOOK" STRATEGIES

The subtle difference between the strategies of "marketing your book" and "marketing *with* your book" is that the latter centers solely on using your book to find new clients or engage new business. While some clients will come to you after they've purchased your book, others can (and will) come in the most expeditious fashion through receiving your book as a gift (from you or someone else).

It's still true (as I mentioned in *You Must Write a Book*), marketing with your book means you're going to give a lot of books away. Much in the same way that, up until the moment you became an author, you've been giving away your business card or handing out marketing folders. Just like business cards, eventually, they end up in the circular file—most likely without any business being transacted. Not so with a book!

When your book is in the hands of a prospect, it will, almost always, get the time and attention it deserves. At the very least, it will have established your credibility and authority, and they are much more inclined to engage you without ever having read your book!

If you are the expert that can solve someone's problem (particularly one that is large or pressing), your book will get at least a cursory read, if not an in-depth look. Let's face it—your book alone can provide the boost of confidence someone needs to inquire about your services.

ALWAYS HAVE A BOOK ON HAND.

The cost of printed books is incredibly low, even hardcover copies with dust jackets. Skeptical? I thought you might be. Think about the cost of a printed paperback—unless you have an especially thick volume, you're going to pay around (including tax and shipping) $4 per book. How much does a client pay you? What's your net? Is it significantly, even exponentially, more than $4? I thought so.

It's worth it to give books away with a huge smile on your face, especially when you consider the potential return on that investment.

As of this printing, I give away hardcover copies of *You Must Write a Book* at the rate of one or two a week. (If I were out networking more, I would give away more.) These hardcover copies cost about $10 per book (including tax and shipping).

I keep a small bag of both paperbacks and hardcovers in my car and put one in my purse with the intention of giving it away *every single time I attend an event*. Most of the time, I do.

AND HAVE A SHARPIE, TOO.

Always offer to sign (using the person's name) and autograph (your best *"John Hancock"*) the books you give away (and if you give a stack to someone to give away, be sure to at least autograph them).

Order a giant box of black Sharpies from Amazon or Office Depot and put them everywhere you'll be asked to sign books (at home, in the office, in your briefcase, and in every household car). Bonus points if you get one in the main color scheme of your book. *You Must Write a Book's* color is red, and this book's color is blue.

You can give your books away as easily as you would a business card, and I encourage you to do so! And you're going to have so much fun meeting readers, signing books to them, and making their day!

I do understand not everyone has a large budget for giving books away. If this describes you, be sure to get a BookFunnel account, follow up on any meetings and connections you make, and directly provide a link for someone to download a digital copy. I promise if you stay focused on marketing and selling your books, over time, you'll have plenty of money to put back into your book business, with a good portion earmarked for gifting books for marketing purposes.

ORDER THEM BEFORE YOU NEED THEM.

I always try to have a dozen or two copies on hand, more if I'm attending a conference or larger event where I would be bummed to run out. When your books arrive, take the time to autograph them, and place a business card inside the front cover. Keep manila envelopes and labels handy so you can quickly mail a book upon request, and if you find yourself without a book, make it the topic of conversation. *I have a book you might like*, preceded with an offer to mail them a copy. My fallback plan is to get the person's mailing address and send them a signed book with a note. An easy way to go from one connection point to two! Be sure to follow up in a week or two to ensure they've received it. Your call or email will serve as a gentle nudge for them to read the book.

BUY THEM IN BULK.

Just as you can sell your books in bulk and enjoy a great profit margin, you can buy them in bulk (as opposed to a dozen or even fifty at a time). Utilizing a printer to print in bulk is a terrific idea and brings down the overall cost of your investment, while simultaneously increasing your profit. Many times, you can turn what would be a book order of 200 into one for 500 with the right printing resource.

SEED YOUR MARKET.

To reap in the fall, you must plant in the spring. Continuously "seeding the market" is my answer to only experiencing spring *once*—because if you continue to seed once you've started, you'll continuously be reaping. Meaning, you'll always have a steady stream of new business flowing through the door!

Hopefully, you've created a 12x12 and have a list of literally dozens of professionals who also interact with your ideal reader, albeit in a different capacity. (The 12x12 is a system I introduced in my networking and business development book, *Business Dating*. It is designed to help you identify networking contacts who can help you increase business.)

Something to consider is that this very list of professionals can benefit from giving your book to their clients (and prospects) as much or more than you do.

*A **quick note on this**.* When a professional you've given your book to passes the book on, there is what I like to call "the trifecta of awesomeness" happening: the person they give the book to wins (they've gotten the gift of great information), the giver wins (they've deepened or accelerated the deepening of their relationship), and you, the author, win (you just might get a new client, too!). Win-win-win—the very best kind, in my book, this book—every book!

So now that you have a stockpile of books and a list of people who could be in your master plan (who are in your 12x12), it's time to get them out into the world as quickly as possible.

Here's a list of ways to prime the pump of ideas—it is by no means complete, yet hopefully, it gets you started:

- Send a copy to each person on the list and offer to send them additional copies to share. *Be sure to provide instructions, such as:* Feel free to share these with your clients. There's more where these came from!

- Send a copy to everyone you mentioned in the book, mark the page(s) where their name appears, and include a note of thanks for their permission to be featured. *If it's a surprise, just include a note about why you included them and maybe even why you admire them.*

- Share copies with service providers—*yours.* Going for your annual physical? Twice-yearly teeth cleaning? Haircut, manicure, or massage? Give a copy to the person who serves you—and their staff—and leave a copy behind in the waiting room. Everyone who provides legal, tax, and financial advice for your business needs a copy, too.

- Traveling for business or personal reasons? Leave a copy in every hotel room, lobby, and coffee shop, in the seat back pocket on airplanes, and in the taxi. Visit local bookstores and see whether they'd like to have a copy (or even stock them).

- Take a copy to your local library (or several). You might even have the chance to teach a workshop in your area of expertise.

- Friends … Do your friends happen to work for companies that would benefit from your book? Would they buy in bulk? Hire you for your expertise? Be willing to share them or even do some seeding in their travels?

- … and Family. Perhaps your wife's alma mater would love to have you become an adjunct professor now that you're an author. Or your husband travels a lot on business—would his clients like a copy of your book?

Seriously, I could continue to write this list for days; your options are only limited to your imagination. Of course, the endgame is that you get traction for your book, countless copies are sold, and you engage millions of dollars in new business, so always look at every tactic to ensure they are part of your bigger strategy.

Now, if you've read this far, I'm hopeful you've come up with some ingenious ideas of your own. Care to share? Send me an email: Honoree@HonoreeCorder.com. I'd love to hear what you've come up with!

Hopefully, I've got your wheels turning, and you've got a list going of the ways you can market *with* your book.

But we're not quite done yet! We've still got some important ground to cover, so after you've jotted down all of your ideas, let's begin!

CHAPTER TEN

IMPROVISE, ADAPT & OVERCOME

We've talked a little about analyzing your marketing activities to see whether they are bearing the desired fruit you'd like. Let's go one more layer deep to ensure you're doing what is really going to work the best. You need to know when to adjust, when to double down, and when to say when.

For the first year after a book launch, I evaluate my MAP every 90 days. My goal is to review the action items I've been doing to see whether they're working, working well, or not. Here's a window into my process.

ANALYZING YOUR MARKETING STRATEGIES

I have a three-part formula for analyzing any marketing strategy, and it is simpler than you think:

1. Am I noticing an increase in sales, or does there seem to be some good momentum?

2. Am I in the black (profitable) after a reasonable period of time?

3. Am I enjoying the process?

Let's break them down, one at a time.

ONE. IS THERE AN INCREASE IN SALES, OR AM I SEEING GOOD, STEADY MOMENTUM?

I know for sure when I do podcast or summit interviews, chances are I'll see a spike in book sales. I make it a point to accept offers to be on almost every podcast (no podcast, for me, is too big or too small), and I'm always on the lookout for a podcast I'd like to be a guest on.

I've spent a lot of time doing things that haven't worked as well, but as an optimist, I choose to see the glass half-full; I learned what didn't work.

It's also important to note that you need to pre-determine how you will define something as successful or unsuccessful.

Case in point: If I spend all day at a trade show and sell five books, that might be seen as a failure. Travel, food, and lodging alone can cost an easy thousand dollars, not to mention the cost of the sponsorship or booth. *However*, if one of those five book purchasers takes one of my courses, joins my mastermind, or hires me to do their book for them, it's a win for sure.

I won't know for sure whether something is a success or a failure for quite some time (maybe even a year or more).

Such a situation would cause me to reflect when contemplating future opportunities and ask some questions:

- Is there a direct line of sight to prospective clients from my activity?
- Does the investment required for my services increase the amount of time it might take a client to engage?
- Is there an easier or more lucrative way to market?

These are the types of questions you'll want to ask yourself *before* you buy into an opportunity—but remember this—you can do your due diligence, make the best possible decision, and still not get your desired outcome. Your desired outcome might take a long period of time to come to fruition.

Or you could hit a bases-loaded home run on the first try. As long as you are thoughtful and intentional, doing the best you can do is all you can do.

TWO. IS A PARTICULAR TACTIC PROFITABLE?

I use AMS (Amazon Marketing Services) to advertise one of my books that's the first in a series. While *sometimes* (most of the time, more than 60% of the time), my ad spend is profitable, it isn't always. Why do I continue? Because readers purchase the other three books in the series. They also purchase the audiobooks or paperbacks, in addition to the e-books. The series sells really well, and I know it sells better when I'm advertising it than when I'm not. (I've tried both; advertising definitely moves the needle.)

I also advertise *You Must Write a Book*, and those ads are not always profitable. If I were analyzing based on book sales alone, I would question the validity of this strategy. But when the other books, courses, and mastermind are factored in, they are indeed worth their weight in gold.

You're not always going to pay $10 and get $100 back from where you spend it—many times, your advertising is a version of planting a seed, and it will eventually grow and return multiplied from a different place.

The way I look at it, the money all goes into the same account. As long as I'm not consistently losing money on something I'm doing, and instead reap some direct and indirect rewards from that original activity, I continue doing it.

Be sure to factor in all of the sources of revenue and expenses that come from your marketing activities.

THREE. ARE WE HAVING FUN YET?

Marketing your book and making sales can be profitable. Marketing with your book and engaging new clients is cause for celebration. But increasing the bottom line isn't your only consideration.

I've mentioned this before, and it bears repeating: You should truly enjoy book marketing. If you have a book marketing strategy in place, and it's yielding results, that's wonderful. But if you dread doing those podcast interviews, or you don't like attending book clubs, *don't do them.*

It's getting more acceptable to talk about mental health these days, so I'm going to add my two cents here.

I cannot stress enough how important it is to keep yourself in a solid, positive place, all while checking every important box: work, family, life, and book marketing.

Please check in with yourself regularly, and make sure you're practicing excellent self-care, even as you check off the items on your Book MAP.

Yes, in case you're wondering, I regularly check in to make sure I'm enjoying what I'm doing. If I'm not having fun, I easily say no. With careful evaluation, you can sell more books while still having lots of fun!

UPDATING YOUR BOOK MARKETING STRATEGY AND PLAN

What works like book marketing magic in the beginning might not be as effective as time passes. When 90 days have passed, and I've discovered a marketing tactic needs a change, I *improvise, adapt,* or *overcome.*

This is a nod to my friends in uniform (thank you for your service), and this method has served me well. It can work for you, too.

Improvise: *to arrange, make, or provide from whatever materials are already available.*

There comes a time when I'm doing something that simply needs a little tweaking. Just as I'm not going to write a new book, I'm not going to throw the marketing baby out with the bathwater.

An example of this would be when Instagram went from static photos to stories, and from stories to videos. I haven't jumped on the video train yet, but I do share my posts (and others' posts) with my stories.

I add in questions, quizzes, music, links, and hashtags. Rarely do your tactics work the same for the entire life of your book. In your evaluation, you'll be able to spot gaps that need to be filled.

Adapt: *to adjust oneself to different conditions, environment, etc.*

As tactics change, so do environments. The one thing that must remain steady is your PMA: **p**ositive **m**ental **a**ttitude. Regardless of conditions, you must keep your mental game in a positive space, keep asking great questions, and acclimate to new conditions.

Overcome: *to prevail; to get the better of a situation.*

Know this: Regardless of the conditions you find yourself and your book in, you can triumph. Keep putting one foot in front of the other, keep talking about your book, and keep smiling.

You've got this!

And finally, *the* **Best Book Marketing Strategy Ever:** And yes, it works like a charm!

Don't shoot the messenger (that's me), but I'm going to share the single best book marketing strategy ever:

Write your next book.

Before you throw this book in the trash, return it, or set it on fire, consider this:

You have a favorite author, right? *Did they write just one book?*

No, probably not. The truth is, one day you discovered the book written by the person who would become your favorite author. You read it. Loved it. Reviewed it. (You did review it, right?) Talked about it. Told your friends and family they had to read it.

Somewhere in there, you went looking to see whether they had any other books you could read. Lo and behold, that same author had written other books. And what did you do? Yup, that's right. You read those books, too. You know you did.

So now someone is reading your book, *and they are loving it!* They told their friends about it, reviewed it, and went looking for more books to read.

Wait, there's only one book? (If there is, that's okay.)

You might want to consider writing your next book. I've written a few, and I can say it gets easier. You write more confidently. The words come easier. The process isn't as overwhelming the second time around.

Most authors end up discovering two things about becoming an author: (1) they love it more than they thought they would, and (2) they have more they want to say.

In another book.

Is this you? I certainly hope so because every book you write will expand your reach and impact.

Our time together has almost come to an end. Before I let you go, I want to give you a challenge. Are you ready?

CHAPTER ELEVEN

BOOK MARKETING CHALLENGE

Now that you've read all the way through the book, the time has come for you to dig into creating your book's marketing action plan—to really capitalize on all that's available to you as an author.

You see, the beauty of being an author isn't solely in book sales. It isn't just in developing new business. It's not found alone in bulk sales, in generating speaking gigs, or even in discovering other new books you can write.

The true beauty is in all of it!

Your book boosts your brand by creating name and face recognition. Just wait until the first time someone says, "Oh! I read your book, and it changed my life!"

Your book brings more business in the door in an easy, fun, and lucrative way. You'll smile to yourself when you cash the first check of a client who called and engaged you without much more than a quick conversation.

Your book establishes you as *the expert*. There will come a time when you hear you were chosen over several other viable candidates because not only are you the best at what you do, your book sealed the deal.

Just having a book is absolutely fantastic! But you must take the book marketing challenge of marketing your book regularly, even daily—just as you brush your teeth, shower, and drink coffee. (Book marketing does require a lot of energy; I recommend all the coffee.)

I've created a short yet powerful challenge to launch you into solid book promotion mode.

Rather than simply completing this book and leaving a great review on Goodreads (please and thank you), while meaning to complete your Book MAP, do these five things instead:

1. Find a buddy, someone who is at the exact same stage as you—maybe even an author who has released a book on a similar topic. Convince them book marketing is the new black and that they need to join you in this challenge.

2. Download your book bonuses and print them out.

3. *Fill them out.* Fill them out by one week from today. Write today's date here: _____. Write one week from today's date here: _____. Exchange MAPs with your buddy—review them, talk through them, make adjustments, and get ready!

4. Take the goals from your MAP, write them on a 3x5 card, and put it on your bathroom mirror, where you'll see your goals every morning.

5. Calendar your book marketing activities for the next 90 days.

What's going to happen? I knew you'd ask that—you are really so smart! What's going to happen is another trifecta of awesomeness.

1. You're going to feel confident that if there's any way for your book to be successful, you will be doing everything you can to make it so.

2. You're going to sell those first 250, then 500, then 1,000, and beyond copies of your book, *and* generate new business in wonderful and somewhat magical ways. (I have it on good authority that preparation + opportunity + action = amazing results.)

3. You're going to look back on deciding to publish your book as one of the top 10 best things you've ever done. *You must just be tempted to write another one,* to which I say, "Do it!"

Let this book be the book that helps you put your book on the map, connects you with people you wouldn't have otherwise connected with, and gets you hired by people who would have missed out on the magic that is you had they not read your book.

What are you waiting for? Let's do this!

AUTHOR'S NOTES

Thank you for reading this book! I had to write it because I meet—almost daily—an author who has a book and is disappointed in the book's performance.

It hasn't sold well. It hasn't generated new business. It didn't lead to other books, new clients, or large royalty checks. But it's not the book's fault; it's no one's fault, really. There is—was—an information gap.

I also wrote this book because I love books, authors, and readers, and I want them to get together much more often.

I used to mistakenly think that only traditionally published authors had a right to sell books, make money, and be well known. As a self-published-only author, I thought I wasn't worthy.

But I kept getting book ideas and felt inspired. So, I kept publishing books.

Almost two decades and dozens of books later, here I am. I hope I am a beacon of light for those who don't feel worthy. I want my words of encouragement to provide a lamp that brightens a path to inspiration and self-assurance.

I want their books—your book—to be a resounding success.

I wrote this book during a personally hard year. I'm a private person, so that's all I will say, folks. But suffice it to say that writing is my happy place, and writing words of encouragement, combined with a process *I know works—it will work for you*—gave me the solace I needed—a place to go when I needed one. I am so glad you were able to join me.

I truly hope that your book finds itself in the hands of those who need it most, and your book benefits you in all of the ways you imagine.

With all of my heart, I wish you happy book marketing.

TODAY IS THE BEST DAY TO MARKET YOUR BOOK!

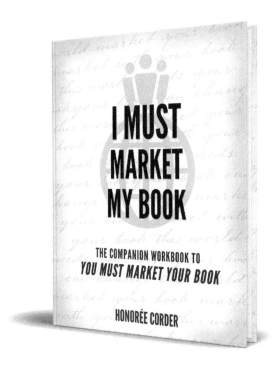

DESIGN YOUR BOOK MARKETING ACTION PLAN AND EXECUTE YOUR BOOK MARKETING LIKE A PRO!

GRAB YOUR COPY TODAY!

QUICK FAVOR

I'm wondering, did you enjoy this book?

Thank you for reading *You Must Market Your Book*. May I ask a quick favor?

Will you please take a moment and leave an honest review on Amazon, Goodreads, or where you purchased the book? Reviews are the single best way to help others discover the book.

Thanks in advance!

GRATITUDE

To my husband, partner, and best friend, Byron. Everything I do is for you, and everything I can do is because of your love and support (and brisket). I love you.

To my BFF, Renee. It's a blessing to have a friend who is there no matter what.

To my team: Karen Hunsanger, Catherine Turner, Brian Meeks, Rob Strasser, and Dino Marino—you rock! It takes a team to bring a book to life and you're my team. I appreciate you more than a few words can express.

To the members of the Empire Builders Mastermind, past and present: you're simply the best and I cherish each and every one of you. Thank you for "all the things."

And to my readers—thank you for reading! I hope your book is a success beyond your wildest dreams (and you'll send me an email and tell me all about it)!

Get a complete book publishing, marketing, and monetization education with these courses.
Visit <u>HonoreeCorder.com/Courses</u>

If you're looking for peer and mentor support
while building your publishing empire,
you'll want to take a look at the
Empire Builders Mastermind.

Learn more at HonoreeCorder.com/Empire

WHO IS HONORÉE CORDER?

Honorée Corder is an empire builder with more than a dozen six- and seven-figure income streams. She's an executive and strategic book coach, a TEDx speaker, and an author of more than 50 books (including *You Must Write a Book*) with over four million books sold worldwide. Honorée passionately mentors aspiring empire builders, coaching them to write, publish and monetize their books, create a platform, and develop multiple streams of income. Find out more at HonoreeCorder.com.

Honorée Enterprises Publishing, LLC
Honoree@HonoreeCorder.com
HonoreeCorder.com
https://www.linkedin.com/in/honoree/
Twitter: @honoree
Instagram: @empirebuilderusa
Facebook: https://www.facebook.com/Honoree